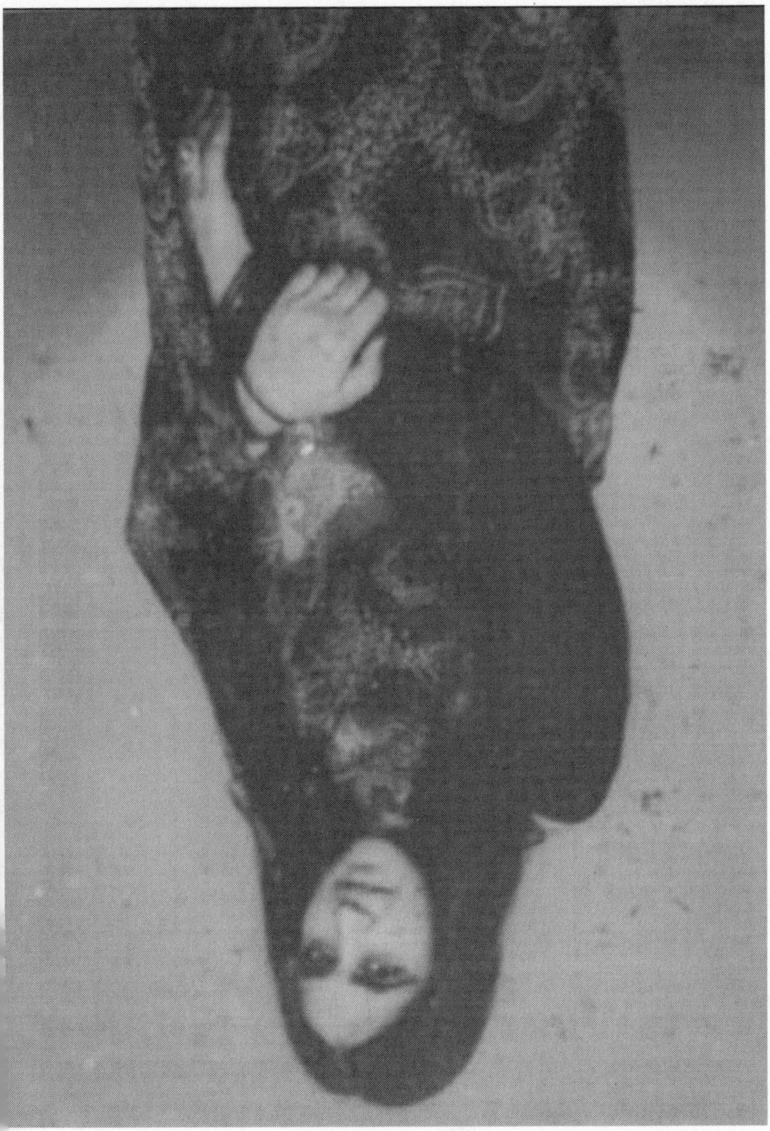

About the Author

WAJIDA TABASSUM (16 March 1935–7 December 2011) lived in the princely state of Hyderabad Deccan, located in south-central India, and was a writer of fiction, verses and songs in Urdu. One of the foremost women writers in the language, she was known for her audacious and semi-erotic stories and her formidable power of storytelling. Her bold writing, through which she took on societal taboos, was seen as immoral and scandalous and faced many a public protest. Otherwise a woman who lived in purdah, Tabassum chose to write about strong and uncomfortable themes that made her 'unpopular' with the Indian society of the mid-1900s.

During the 1960s and 1970s, her stories were published in India in many magazines. Her books include *Teh Khana*, *Kaise Samjhaoon*, *Phul Khilne Do*, *Zakhm-e-Dil Aur Mahak Aur Mahak*, and *Zan, Zar, Zameen*, which was her last work, published in 1989. Her story titled 'Utran' (Cast-offs) was televised as a popular soap opera of the same name in India in 1988.

About the Translator

REEMA ABBASI is a resident of Karachi, Pakistan. She is an independent contributor to several leading newspapers and a commentator on socio-political issues. She has been a journalist with the *News International*, *Herald Magazine* and *Dawn*, and is the author of *Historic Temples in Pakistan: A Call to Conscience* and *Ajmer Sharif: Awakening of Sufism in South Asia*. Reema has been a recipient of the Gender in Journalism Award in 2003 by UNESCO and the Rajiv Gandhi Award for the Literary Personality of the Year at the Fifth Rajiv Gandhi Excellence Awards in 2014. Throughout her career, Reema's writings have focused on marginalized communities, socio-political concerns, heritage and the values of secularism. Her other passions include travel, arts and culture.

SIN

STORIES BY WAJIDA TABASSUM

TRANSLATED BY REEMA ABBASI

hachette
INDIA

First published in 2021 by Hachette India
(Registered name: Hachette Book Publishing India Pvt. Ltd)
An Hachette UK company
www.hachetteindia.com

3

Cover design by Pia Alize Hazarika

ISBN 978-93-91028-88-6

For sale in all territories excluding Pakistan.

Hachette Book Publishing India Pvt. Ltd
4th & 5th Floors, Corporate Centre,
Plot No. 94, Sector 44, Gurugram 122003, India

Typeset in Dolly Pro 11/16
by R. Ajith Kumar, New Delhi

Printed and bound in India
by Manipal Technologies Limited

MIX
Paper from responsible sources
FSC www.fsc.org FSC™ C043100

To

The late Anjum Chhatari-Abbasi. Devoted social worker for dispossessed women and challenged children.

My Amma.

Wajida Tabassum and her courage.

Translator's Note

> 'Women have been called queens a long time, but the kingdom given them isn't worth ruling.'
>
> – Louisa May Alcott, *An Old-Fashioned Girl* (1869)

For a woman, life in a traditionally conservative South Asian society has always been a fierce battle for purity.

In a drab, dimly lit, smoky bistro, she may be pictured as dishevelled and alone, licking rice from her greasy hands. Thick, murky streaks of curry run down her chin and stain her blouse. A messy table before her is the evidence of her sins – sins of hedonism and indulgence. But the visual belies her reality. She is still hungry and dissatisfied. Framed as either banal or brazen, forever shamed for her desires, she has been carefully placed between rapture and revulsion through the ages.

Wajida Tabassum's voice is of and for these women. It breaks down the social confines of virtue that refuse women their right to possess the base elements of human nature – lust, envy, greed, wrath – and condemn them to lifelong rites of self-

denial. The notions that imprison them cannot sustain pretence for long. Eventually, they often cast aside fears of *jannat se jala watni* – banishment from Paradise – a deeply instilled concern in orthodox households.

Their journey out of environs that revel in women's submission and deprivation is the primary focus of Wajida's stories that go against the grain with protagonists who claim and indulge in the primal. She is startlingly clear in what she portrays – all that is a sin to others is salvation to her women.

In the 1950s, Wajida's work was viewed as explosive, unorthodox and impure. From a respectable, conservative, but poor home, Wajida Tabassum, in her early twenties, was reviled for her non-conformist, semi-erotic work. Old-fashioned Hyderabad Deccan saw her as an impure menace, determined to shock, lead women astray and tarnish the family name. When her stories – which she used to post in letters to newspapers and various magazines – began appearing regularly, they were noticed by the people in her hometown of Amravati.* Her relatives came together to bar her from writing and her correspondence began to be severely monitored at home. Despite these excruciating circumstances, Wajida

---

* Wajida Tabassum's hometown is 'Amrauti' in the Urdu text of 'Meri Kahaani' (My Story). Amravati is a village near Faizabad, now Ayodhya, and another Amravati is a town in Maharashtra. During the partition, the family moved to Hyderabad Deccan. According to Wajida's own account, the journey took thirteen days, so we can conclude that 'Amrauti' is Amravati in Maharashtra.

persevered, writing and posting stories to newspapers and magazines. However, when further confronted by her enraged family, fear forced her to renounce some of her work. This was the time when Jilani Bano, Krishan Chander, Ismat Chughtai and Saadat Hasan Manto were established giants of Urdu literature. It was ironic that Wajida's relatives and distant kin who were familiar with the bold and unconventional writing of other women writers had a rabid view of her own work and used Chughtai's writing – despite her fame and stature – as a jibe to knock Wajida's progress.

As the stories flowed to the masses, she faced death threats and mobs took to the streets to torch the offices of her publishers. In staunch resistance, even though by now she faced abject poverty, Wajida wrote and chronicled debauchery in aristocratic homes and took on middle-class taboos with astonishing nerve and in lyrical prose. Other than her popular short story 'Utran' (Hand Me Downs) that was made into a television soap, Wajida Tabassum's body of work remains an untouched jewel of Urdu literature. This is therefore the first volume of translations of her writing into English, containing nineteen intrepid short stories. These stories seek to capture the entire range of the realities of middle-class compulsions and the depravities indulged in by the social elite.

The four sections in this volume deal with dark, debauched and tragic aspects of life and are structured on the theme of the 'deadly sins', namely lust, pride, greed and envy. Sensually treated accounts of jealousy, desire, injustice and suppression,

they signal a theatre of discontent with clever charades of symbolism. Wajida captures the power of the subliminal and the subconscious with precision and subtlety. Themes of impotence, powerplay, betrayal and abandonment run through most of the stories. They almost serve as quiet metaphors for the downfall of the nobility.

The story of her life in her own words, 'Meri Kahaani', written when she was twenty-four, forms the centre of this volume. It provides insight into her work and is an exquisite testament of a bold and original writer.

Stories such as 'Hor Upar!' came under heavy fire from critics for the unapologetic depiction of a Begum's revolt against her husband's drunken sexual escapades with maids in the palace. Spurned and lustful, she appoints a young boy to massage her. Her gharara, a garment stitched between the thighs, is soon replaced by a lehenga, a long skirt, a signal for him to move upwards, past her knees. The scene in which his hands gradually ascend, causing a slow rise to the crescendo, bears a subtle resemblance to one in Chughtai's *Lihaaf*. The Begum's refusal to acknowledge any threat of censure forms the rest of the story.

In her stories, Wajida Tabassum employs nuance to a limited degree – just enough to create an explosion. 'Tauba Tauba' is a tale built around an expression of coyness and purity as its title suggests. The writer takes an atypical view of its perception and impact, and we see the two-word expression eat away at the virility of the protagonist from his childhood. His first arousal

was sudden as a little boy. The story is spun around a cold marriage and the boy's guilt and inner conflict, increasing as he grows older. In its climax, Wajida uses notes of smell, sweat, a worn-out sari and a broom as subliminal clues to identify the void in him. She defines it as his quest for rawness and an escape from the net of 'Tauba Tauba'.

Despite all the social chains, Wajida surprises her readers with her own fearlessness. She navigates the darker, seamy alleys of her imagination and craft with tales such as 'Rozi ka Sawaal', 'Chhinaal' and 'Ladki Bazaar'.

'Chhinaal' and 'Ladki Bazaar' are forceful indictments of societal excesses towards women, whereas 'Rozi ka Sawaal' is as visceral as it is desperate in the squalor of an indigent sex district. However, its women cling to their individuality and their dreams. Shalu, a feisty character in the story, and a personal favourite, is a girl who fights to woo her customers in the hope of acquiring a home of her own. Her character is perfumed with an innocence amid the perilous circuit of her world. The untarnished purity of her fantasy is evident in her fresh and unjaded voice. Even the tricks she turns are not more than little white lies.

The destiny of age-old symbols of patriarchal sway – in this instance a nose ring – changes hands with immaculate pluck in 'Nath ka Ghuroor'. Young Sharafat Dulhan is encumbered with an ill-tempered, cold and impotent Nawab Wajahat. Born into a religious family, she has been raised only to surrender. A docile girl's transformation into a woman in command and

completely cognisant of her physical needs as well as her status, the story navigates alarming twists and aspects of misogyny perpetrated by older women on their younger counterparts. Deliciously scandalous events create a new woman who seals her place and power in the royal clan. She also trades the husband's defeat with her emancipation from celibacy and childlessness.

'Lungi Kurta' is another deft metaphor for cold wrath and revenge. The tale is wrapped around garments. A new, happy bride who finds herself caught amid and then betrayed by a mere exchange of clothes makes her own, lethal move.

Perhaps the most tragic story in this collection is 'Kaalay Baadal'. For most, it will be interpreted as a couple's greed for more money. For me, the adamant possessiveness cast in the wife's deep, consuming love for her husband manifests in the tragic fate of their child.

Sin, like people, has shades and facets. 'Faakhta' is an aspect in the psychology of greed that is not acquisitive but aspirational. It is a simple sense of longing. Psychologists call it a 'greed for love', seen as the mere presence of the object of love in the beholder's mind. Maina, a free-spirited, self-assured young girl with little regard for convention and societal sanction, is the axis of the story. She disregards the context of the man she eyes and his benign association with her. A woman's defiant gaze of attachment and the social boundaries she pushes for it guide the story.

Similarly, 'Dhanak ke Rang Nahin' depicts the many forces of envy. The story became immensely popular at the time of its

publication. The undercurrents and strains of relationships, the familiar ordinariness of the central male lead and his bonds with the people around him possibly resonated strongly among readers as vital dynamics in the experience of their lives.

In much the same way, the unmistakable realism of 'Talaq, Talaq, Talaq' and its resonance with developments around the issue of women's rights in present-day South Asia suggests that the world hasn't changed all that much since it was written.

Most of Wajida Tabassum's women belong to or are located in conservative, demanding households. Wajida sets them free to feast on their desires and emotions. Her language is fine-drawn – the artistry with which she weaves the layers of denied, smothered feelings is as forceful as the ultimate implosion, usually one of shattering voltage. The stories are landscapes of shifting passions and, in the end, the triumph of the self.

The idea to translate Wajida's work into English came from my desire to bring to a wider audience the voices of Wajida's women, their silent despair and eventual detonation. Like Wajida, her women are rebels who liberate themselves. Unafraid of judgement, opinion and even desertion, they chase their freedom with a stubborn passion.

I selected these stories* because they, like a deep, profound

---

*List of books consulted for the Urdu text of the stories:

1. Mahmood, Tariq, comp. *Wajida Tabassum ke Afsane*. Lahore: Book Talk, 2010.
2. Tabassum, Wajida. *Sheher-e-Mailedmnoon Afsane*. Lahore: Sang-e-Meel Publications, 2014.
3. Munir, Salman, comp. *Wajida Tabassum ke Anmol Afsane*. Lahore: Abdullah Academy, 2010.

alto, struck the gut and reverberated in the heart. As women who have been conditioned to be stoic and accepting on the most part, we are on a perpetual quest to find our voice and the courage to express what we really feel. In my journey as a journalist, I have come across many women confined by the same strife and limits as Wajida – bereft of a mission or ambition, they exist in the haze of misery, numb and silent. Wajida's furious persistence in the pursuit of equality for the women in her stories connects with stunning precision to the dilemmas that confront women in modern times. Challenging patriarchal power structures to find a definitive balance can only emerge from similar conviction and grit.

However, this translation is also a labour of love. Wajida spoke not just to a small voice in me but also to the context of most women, privileged or not. It was challenging, as one had to be true to her emotions, those of the characters and their stories. In doing so, I have adapted the elaborate descriptive aspects of the stories so that the force of their rendition remains undiluted for readers in English. The hope is that, through this translation (and hopefully more to come), Wajida Tabassum and her oeuvre will find space in mainstream culture as a powerful commentary on socio-political predicaments in the times that we live in and serve the cause of gender justice with the vigour of a cannonball, so that the shells that imprison women may be cracked wide open.

Reema Abbasi
Karachi, 2021

Contents

Ek Baat

A Word

'Torment is universal. It does not spare a soul. Why should you worry and weep over it, or declare it to the world? When you tell the world about it, you erase everything learnt from it and gained through it.'

These lines, and Dagh Dehlvi's verse, '*Shirkat e gham bhi nahin chahti ghairat meri...* (My pride does not want a consoler)' stared at me before I wrote 'My Story'.

I spent endless hours wondering whether my circumstances should be disclosed. In doing so, do I risk a loss? Did it ever return anything?

Then I thought, I must write regardless of the perils. As for '*shirkat e gham*', my grief wore a shroud because I knew the futility of laying it bare.

My sadness has become my past. I want to tell my tale because you questioned my writing. My life does not shame me.

Wajida Tabassum

29 December 1959

Hyderabad Deccan

Lust

1

Chhinaal

Fallen Venus

Sabir, the spoilt scion of a wealthy family, first saw her at a friend's wedding. Agra's Gauhar Jaan was to perform the *mujra*, a common rite of celebration and a testimony to grandeur in stately homes. The poetic bows, tinkling of anklets, twirls against golden drapes were seals of splendour.

For days on end, a battle raged in his mind. 'How can I lose my heart to a nautch girl who serves hearts and bodies? How?'

'This Agra girl, my God, she has my heart in a knot,' he would say to his friend Anwer over and over again.

Finally, Anwer took him for a round of the brothel. A perfect setting where literary descriptions of nautch abodes

came alive – a madame, a tutor, musicians, seated on ivory sheets, against plush, velvet bolsters.

Gauhar Jaan, a vision of exquisiteness and conceit, knew the art of seduction. She teasingly slipped out of his gaze and walked over to the jeweller waiting with all his gems on exhibit. She picked up pieces with disdain and put them aside as if they were acerbic fruit, until her interest lingered on a ring.

'Dear, I have had it with your whining for a ring. Do you like this one? Take it,' said the madame, Baiji, giving her prized patron Akbar Seth an indulgent glance.

'Take it. Only diamonds for these fingers,' Seth encouraged.

'I am not so worthy,' sighed Jaan with rehearsed innocence.

'My dear, a thousand rupees are mere pittance compared to your worth. Take it.'

In no time, the jeweller had spread out all his rings before Jaan, each of which cost twelve thousand rupees. They glittered like stardust as she tried them on, fitting her as if crafted especially for her fingers.

Seth flung his visiting card at the gemsman. 'Take my name and collect your money from my shop.'

A little later, a fawning audience settled in, the lights dimmed and she appeared behind a tissue curtain. Gauhar bowed in an *adaab* and the luminous spray of her rings shone through the curtain. Sabir sat intoxicated by her beauty.

'Worlds separate us. I must search for love at another threshold, alas,' said Sabir's heart. But he had no say over it.

Anwer interrupted his reverie. 'Prostitutes have the same eyes for everyone, but they don't fall in love. Money is their religion. Why get caught in this deception? You can never tell how the one you celebrate as yours sees other men.'

Jaan's coy ways and muted guile were etched in Sabir's heart. Early the next day, he left for her brothel on his own, and was the first to arrive there. She sat resplendently on a spread with gold star trails. The red drapes in the room were still in their covers. He took his place a little away from her.

'Ah, they are blessed,' he gushed, looking at her slippers.

Fazed by his brash remark, Gauhar Jaan receded. 'You are so brazen.'

Her displeasure stole his breath. 'As bashful as women in noble homes... she has all the ornaments of a chaste woman,' he thought.

And then he moved closer. 'For God's sake, don't try me so much.'

'Why do you make claims you cannot stand by? Will *huzoor* really die?'

'Am I alive to you?'

She let out a laugh that fell on him like lightning, a laugh that could set lush fields on fire if it came from the firmament.

'You laugh? Am I a liar?'

'Look under your collar, search within.'

'Let me look under yours. There isn't much under mine,' Sabir said mischievously. She blushed and covered her face. 'God! You are so shameless. Who says such things?'

Her demure ways held his universe. Their few trysts became the centre of his existence, the last of which consumed him like an inferno. But Anwer and other friends still saw his love as a fleeting fascination and spoke about her with disdain. They told him that quiet wiles destroyed more homes than shameless whores ever did.

'No, she is for the home. How did she ever get caught in this ghastly trade!' was his constant protest.

Every year, a celebration at his friend's lavish home had a courtesan as its centre piece. This time, the invite carried Gauhar Jaan's name. Sabir watched her till dawn, fixated on her with an eagle's gaze. She pushed the harmonium aside as the muezzin cleared his throat for the call to prayer at sunrise. Some, devoured by the nightlong vigil, collapsed at the host's, others dragged themselves homewards. Musicians stretched like sleepy stray dogs on mattresses covered in white with rows of pillows arranged on them.

Sabir found a place by Gauhar Jaan's feet. He'd only slept a few hours when cold hands pressed against his soles. 'A muslin shirt and bare feet? Such sleep is dangerous,' her syrupy voice poured into his ears. He lay there quietly as she wrapped his cold feet in her shawl.

Could his tumultuous heart wield such power that

her heartbeat was now in sync with his? Sabir's mind was inundated with questions and thoughts of his mother, who was an unyielding ritualist. She prayed five times a day, observed fasts, and went into seclusion during Ramzan.

'I always say, a whore, like chickenpox, cannot stay inside the house,' roared Amma Bi, when he got home and stated his intention to marry Gauhar Jaan. She slammed her *paandaan*, kicked the *paan* basket and glared at Sabir with incensed eyes. The hang of his face made him a portrait of abject anguish.

'After all, this is a tainted woman from a brothel. Her kind cut and run within seconds. If you send someone to check her room, it will take her only minutes to clean it out and escape with another customer!'

'Amma...' His sister Zehra feebly attempted to stop her from talking further.

'Unimaginable. A cheap slut in this home? They destroy homes, how can she nurture one? My Sabir could only find a hooker,' his mother lamented.

In that moment, if someone slashed Sabir open, his veins would run dry. He still tried to stir the staunch believer in her. 'Amma, the one who asks for forgiveness is as pure and sinless as a newborn. If she wants to discard a life of deceit and riches, is God not leading her out of sin? If He wants to rescue her, do you want to disobey Him?'

'Son, feet that know the thrills of a *mujra* cannot be still within the four walls of a home. How can a woman who

has seen countless men, be satisfied by just one? I know. A whore, like chickenpox, cannot be contained.' Amma Bi was merciless.

Finally, the headstrong Sabir gave up all thought of coaxing his stubborn mother and decided to take on his family and their Syed community.

He was Amma's sole heir; Zehra was to be married in a few months. The thought of losing her son haunted Amma Bi, but whether it would be to poison or to Gauhar Jaan, however, was in her hands. So, Amma Bi relented. Gauhar Jaan crossed their threshold as Dulhan Begum and Zehra welcomed her with all the warmth and joy. But Amma was determined to char her happiness with ridicule. 'A whore, like chickenpox, doesn't stay inside.'

'Please, Amma, don't do this now.'

'If, for you, a sullied woman is a *shareefzadi*, then why give another name to a harlot?' she bit back.

The next morning, Dulhan woke before sunrise to the sounds of Amma's ablutions, coughing, her loud recital of scriptures and Zehra's holy rituals. Sabir, satiated after a night of flaming passion and alcohol, was deep in sleep.

'Oh Lord, have I come to my husband's home or to a mosque?' was her first thought at the first light of her new life. She took a stroll in her elaborate bedroom and its marble terrace. Blooms of all shades lined the ledges, with a seating arrangement on the side. Her rebirth sank in and she smiled.

Dulhan gave Sabir a gentle nudge. '*Huzoor*, wake up.' Her own words startled her. These were terms of her old home. Her language, like her, had to transform. 'Listen, time to wake up. Don't you have to make a living?' she tried again.

After breakfast, Gauhar and Zehra skipped up the stairs to the roof to dry their long hair. On the opposite roof, their neighbour sat with a book. He recognized Dulhan Begum from a *mujra* gathering and scanned her like a searchlight, then whistled. Begum raised her head and he flirted with a snigger. 'Darling, what brought you to this roof? Your wet hair? I have ample muscle and money. Why not my house?'

Discomfort turned Zehra to stone. Dulhan felt her skin melt away. She pulled Zehra aside and said, 'We will not come here again. They are an indecent lot.' As the two rushed down, he yelled, 'You are as used as the flaccid remains of a flower. My queen, let me get to know this fresh bud.'

Dulhan ran to her room and dove onto her bed in tears. 'I should not be here. I am not worthy. My presence can cast a dark shadow on your life, Bibi.'

'Bhabi, don't say that.' Zehra placed her hand on Dulhan's lips. 'They are the scum of our neighbourhood. We don't meet them. The other neighbours are more supportive and affectionate than our relatives,' she placated her sister-in-law.

'You will not understand. I know. Even if my infamy doesn't stalk me, my misfortune is mine, like my shadow,' Dulhan wept.

'Please stop, Bhabi, or I will cry with you.'

Days went by. Dulhan basked in Sabir's love despite Amma Bi's lacerating silence. But their long, lustful hours in their room were often broken by her thoughts. She felt the matriarch's eyes on their door burn holes in her. The grand dame had not shared the dining table with her even once after their marriage. Meanwhile, Zehra spent her days in school and Dulhan immersed herself in household chores, occasionally sending Sabir on mundane errands.

Zehra's routine dash for the stairs as soon as she returned from school sparked Amma's usual tirade against Sabir. 'You have ruined your life. You had no concern for your sister. She spends her time with your whore. I never let her go to the roof. Now she is there with that streetwalker.'

Dulhan was always bewildered by the blame. 'Why is the onus on me? Zehra is never with me.'

One afternoon at lunch, Sabir said he would return late that night because of an office meeting. After dusk, Zehra pranced into Dulhan's room. 'My lovely Bhabi, please let me wear your sari with black and green flowers.'

'You don't have to ask. My belongings are yours.'

Everyone ate dinner, but Dulhan stayed hungry, waiting for her husband. As the house grew warm, she moved to the roof, where she sensed a strange indulgence in the air. It hung like a winding sheet. Then, rushed movements and slow whispers rose from behind the water tank on the notorious neighbour's roof.

'How did you make it today?'

'My brother will be late.'

'And if he is early...?'

'I am not so innocent. I have his wife's sari. If Amma or he catch a glimpse, they will think it's Bhabi. Her being a prostitute is rather good for us.'

'But I want to make love, I am serious. I can't take these furtive meetings any more. Now let me!'

'We will. Thanks to her sari.'

'Don't toy with me.'

'I want it too.'

'Wonderful that your brother brought a prostitute home. We can ravage each other till your wedding and then when you visit.'

In that instant, Gauhar knew she had been born twice. In her first birth, she was the most precious commodity of a brothel. In her second, she was to return to it. In between, she unhinged her heart. She made a quiet return to her room.

Dear Zehra,

Please tear this letter after you read it.

May God keep you happy and on the righteous path. You are engaged and I wish you a happy marriage soon.

I have understood your love for my saris. My life is behind me. It passed the way it was meant to. However, as your brother's wife, the days of honour spent in this

home make it my duty to guide you and stop you from straying. What really is the value of a whore? My infamy, like an old, loyal maid, will never leave me. But I will not stand witness to you tainting your character.

Dear child, if you use my clothing, it is my clothing that will get sullied as it has in the past. But, all the holy water will fail to wash away the stains on the fabric of your life. Tread the pious path ordained by your faith and home. This is my advice and prayer for you.

I came to this house with my head lowered to this house. Ever since, only Sabir's body, the wind, the rays of the sun and moonbeams have touched my body. As I leave, every fragment of my being will bear the imprints of your brother's incomparable love. Once again, I leave this pure love with a lowered head, so you can stand tall for the rest of your life.

Your Bhabi.

'I always said a whore, like chickenpox, can never stay inside.' Amma slammed her *paandaan*, kicked her basket of *paan* aside, and pinned Sabir with a knowing look. 'A whore stayed a whore. Did she not?'

2

Hor Upar!

Up, further up!

The skin has never lied.

Nawab Sahab cut an unsteady silhouette as he stumbled out of the servants' quarters and dragged himself towards the bedroom, his breath bitter with alcohol and body sweetened by the scent of jasmines. He collapsed onto his luscious bed. Every gilded crevice of this stately room was covered in odours of seduction.

Pasha Dulhan awoke to the stench of betrayal and leapt to his side, simmering like an ember.

'I want the truth! Don't lie! Where were you? Were you with a whore?' she yelled as desperation crept over her.

His hearty laugh cut her rant short. His response sliced through her. 'Where is the need for me to lie? What you suspect is the truth.'

'Have you been with Gul Badan?' she asked.

'When you know, why ask?' he replied.

Trembling with rage, hatred and sadness, Pasha Dulhan became a furnace of tears and anger. Objects crashed against the bedroom walls as she rued her fate.

'My parents destroyed my life! They gave me to a man untouched by shame or remorse. Every man strays, but mine throws it in my face. He says, "Why ask if you know?" How many women does he need? His ravenous lust knows no bounds! Keep your palace and give me a divorce before this night passes. This disgrace, this life...'

She wanted to run, to take herself, her memories, her ghosts, all her traces away from him. Her anguish was now swirling in a saline deluge.

But, warmed by a woman's body and lulled by alcohol, Nawab Sahab had long sunk into deep slumber.

Pasha Dulhan's pale nights turned to white days bathed in monochromatic monotony. She had come to the palace as a bride of under twenty years, a stranger to conjugal intimacy and mundane niceties. In the nights of their youth, Nawab Sahab's skin had ached for her touch; that touch of servitude. But when he would ask her to massage his legs, she'd flip to the other side and order a young maid to do his bidding.

'You be at his feet. I am sleepy,' she would say.

Morning rays awakened them in joy. Time after time, the same plea stumbled out of his mouth. 'Begum, please massage my legs sometimes. These *haraamzadis* lack the touch I crave.'

His wish rarely failed to draw a retort from Pasha Dulhan. 'Listen to your new demands! Is that my worth? A flock of maids was sent with me to perform such menial chores.'

Begum's sleep deepened with each night. The Nawab immersed himself in the quicksand of darkness and its fires.

But Pasha Dulhan began to welcome the day with eyes wide open; slowly the sheath of the dark hours of the night slipped away. His coldness, her being untouched by her own Nawab, sent knives through her core. Loneliness assumed the form of an apparition that never left her side.

The body pines like the stomach craves. Yet a bride soaked in intoxicating fragrance no longer made Nawab Sahab's heart race. She would often lie awake in an icy, bare bed. And in Hyderabad Deccan's renowned Nawab Riyasat Yar Jung's palace, to search for him was a mere fantasy. Just one round of its grounds turned her legs to pulp.

Ashen nights made her attentive to whispers of married friends. She learnt that when a husband didn't return to his marital bed, when weeks went by unlit by his passions, something else was burnt to dust – his wife, their home and marriage. But she had to be the graveyard of these

revelations. How could she tell someone that her Nawab was consumed by other girls? Besides, Pasha Dulhan knew that men strayed when their wives didn't keep them captivated, or plenty wouldn't be fastened to ageing wives. She was her own curse and captive.

One night, some years and a few children into their marriage, she waited for Nawab Sahab. He swayed in with black stains on his face – residues of a night of betrayal, of a woman's kohl. Alas, the charcoal of sin.

She flashed across the room like an eagle to its prey. Tracing the marks with her fingers, she asked, 'How did you get this blackness on your face?'

Unfazed, as was expected of his position, his reply reeked of apathy. 'This damn Mehru lathers her eyes with *kajal*. It must have rubbed off.' In an instant, Pasha Dulhan turned into a limp heap of despair.

She was ready for a commotion, to hurl expletives, unleash her demons and slay his soul. But Nawab Sahab's stolid words left nothing to be said.

From this moment, the cacophony, the pomp and circumstance, the revelry of the palace fell silent for her. Pasha Dulhan, once the axis of this frenetic world, receded from the galaxy she was meant to rule.

Coursing with spite, her heart ached to see the flock of nubile maids banished. Her mind defied reason. But with the social compulsions that bound her, a revolt against

tradition was beyond her power. Ladies of her noble rank would make petty fodder of her home. She could almost hear them cackle, 'What is the worth of nobility that is without staff?'

Aches of the heart spread to the bone; her head pounded, spine hurt, knots shot through her feet, a certain spasm gripped her being. Weariness began to writhe all over her body. A naturopath of renown was summoned. In a regal home of conservative Hyderabad, Hakiman Amma had to accompany him to survey symptoms. Hakim Sahab's only allowed transgression was to check Dulhan's pulse.

Pasha Dulhan's symptoms betrayed her malaise.

'Where does Nawab Sahab sleep?' asked the old hakim.

'In the mardana,' replied Hakim Amma on the patient's behalf.

He took a long pause, knowing that he could afford neither candour nor silence. Then, he gave Pasha Dulhan a bottle of oil to be used for a daily massage. Pasha Dulhan was adamant not to let the maids near her. Their sight sent tides of fury through her and she spewed venom. Finally, she picked a young adolescent boy from the palace staff for her services. He could hardly be a threat to her virtue she reckoned.

Nawab Sahab and Pasha Dulhan's raging arguments had become an everyday affair. They almost reached the brink of parting. The Nawab had turned more brazen. 'Today I slept

with this one, I cavorted with that one! What can you say?' he would slur aloud.

She cursed and bit. In hushed tones, she even professed to him her own body's longings. Nawab Sahab was aghast. '*Allah mian* knew a man needed more sex and allowed four wives. If it were the same for women, then why wasn't it permitted for them?' he threw back at her.

Their veil of pretence was in tatters. And his deafening argument robbed her of a voice. That morning, when she picked up a bottle of jasmine oil for her mane, it slid out of her hands and broke. The oil streamed across the floor. Exasperated, she called out to Gul Badan: 'It's going to waste, slap it on your hair.' That night the scent of jasmine wafted over Nawab Sahab's body.

People in those days confined women within unnatural notions – of asexual virtues and deadened sexual impulses. As a woman crossed thirty, she transformed into another self. And this was a time when Pasha Dulhan was in celestial splendour, as ripe as a rising moon, every pore set to crackle.

Her body, moist as a wet monsoon night, was tauter than a maestro's sitar strings. 'Your touch is so light, I need force,' she moaned.

The boy, barely fourteen years of age, was so weary of her stature that his touch was cautious. Once through with a back and head massage, he would slink to her feet, tired hands pressing her calves with all their vigour.

The haveli women dressed in traditional voluminous kurtas and churidar pyjamas; the young draped ghararas and the saree was a scarce sight. Pasha Dulhan's tight pyjama kept his hands at her soles, so she began to wear ghararas that made her calves easy to reach. One rainy afternoon, she sent for the chief chef, a moment of honour for any servant of the haveli.

'Give this boy Rehmat more nutrition with *ghee parathas* for breakfast. He is too weak to give good massages,' she ordered.

Eyes fixed on her face, chest swelling in concert with rapid breaths, apprehensive oil-drenched hands shifted the beautiful brocade of her gharara with fears of tarnishing them. Rehmat's determined strokes were met with, 'Up, further up.' Porcelain calves shone like mirrors. He gazed in awe, often afraid to see his reflection in their glaze.

One night, Pasha Dulhan's pain stung as her muscle contractions stiffened. 'Up, further up. It's killing me, I'm feverish. Go up to my knees,' she said, as she twisted with a groan.

Rehmat's rich diet of a *ghee*-laced cuisine, dry fruits and meat gave him sizzling daydreams. An unfamiliar warmth rose in him. 'Up, further up...' knees, creamy, tender like coconut meat, made his skin tingle. He closed her legs with a jolt.

'You are defying my orders,' said Pasha Dulhan, raising her head to look his way. She scanned Rehmat for the first

time. He peered hard into her eyes and turned away. There sat a pulsating, firm young man, plucked from an array of workers, because the depraved group of maids had eyes only for her husband.

At this very moment, slack-jawed and slumping over, Nawab Sahab trundled into the room. Not intoxicated enough to bear the sight of a boy sitting by his wife's feet, he roared, 'This bastard, here?'

Rehmat fled like the wind, but Begum did not shy away from a spirited response. 'Why are you concerned? This is my business!'

'For the sake of all that you hold holy, tell me, who was that boy?' the Nawab bellowed.

'For years, you have had a new girl caress you, massage you and do so much more! If I have someone treat my pain, you want an explanation?'

'A man is like that rug in the courtyard, many feet walk over it and their marks are overlooked. But a woman is a pristine white sheet. Her purity is marred by a faint stain.'

Pasha Dulhan struck back. 'Oh Lord! Your honour, your glory! How, with your soiled lap, do you have the audacity to bring up so many names for me? You couldn't find anything else, so you have created such an uproar over a boy?'

'He's not a boy. Get him married and he'll become a father in no time. He is not to cross this doorsill!'

'And if he does?'

'Then I will divorce you!'

'Give it to me this moment!'

The room fell silent like a tomb. After thirteen years of marriage, terms of endearment and respect lay eroded by bitterness. But never before had Nawab Sahab's begum given such an assured, intrepid response to his threat.

Worse ensued; she twisted her vengeful knife deeper.

'After our divorce, all of Hyderabad will know that you cannot be with a woman, that you are impotent. You are not even the father of my children. Now free me from this life and give me a divorce. I have suffered in this haveli, now it is my time to bask in joy before your eyes.'

Her revolt was beyond the man's imagination. But he was determined to keep his head up, his eyes burning holes in her.

The morning sun saw a silken Pasha Dulhan adorned in a shimmering saree over a lehenga. Rehmat arrived for his daily service and his carnal gaze locked on her.

'Why are you just looking at me? Are your hands drained of strength?' she demanded, interrupting his reverie.

He lifted up her lehenga. 'You call this a massage? Move up.' He sensed a flirtatious note in her reproach.

As his ears began to blush with the rising heat of his body, her encouragements of 'Move up, further up' rang loud.

Then again, 'Up, further up.'

She traced the contours of his pubescent frame with her eyes as he kneaded her legs in slow, distracted motion.

Pulling up the deep purple garment – 'Umm, up, further up.'

'More... Further up.'

'Move up, *hor upar*!'

With a frenzied swing he sent the bowl of sandalwood oil flying in the air, and covered her, moving high up...filling her till there was no space left to go 'up, further up' any more. Saturated in the sultry aroma of sandalwood, Pasha Dulhan was fresh as dew the next morning. Nawab Sahab had returned after dawn and slipped into their bed. Rehmat bent down to present a glass of water on a silver tray to him. As his master moved closer to take the glass, he smelt the same perfume. Nawab Sahab turned to look at his wife spread across the bed, a cascade of black tresses covering her pillow. She beamed with the glee of a conqueror.

'You have to leave for the village tomorrow. They need a *munshi*,' he said to Rehmat.

'As you wish, Sarkar...'

Nawab returned the smile of a victor to Pasha Dulhan.

Two hours later, her skin and soul as exuberant as her desire, the Begum swooped down into the royal kitchen with instructions for the chef.

'Mama Bi, you know Zubaida's son Sharfu? Give him elaborate meals. He will massage me from now. I need strong hands.'

Mama Bi complied at once. Sharfu was served velvety egg *halwa* that shone with a healthy layer of ghee.

3

Ladki Bazaar

The Flesh Market

As the *azaan* ended, Nawab Habib Yar Jung broke his fast with fine scotch. A sharp-eyed maid, with a pronounced swagger, carried a tray laden with succulent kebabs to him. She used her curves well as she winded her way out.

He summoned another minion with a clap; head bowed, the servant scurried in.

'Where is Mirza Sahab? Dead?' he roared.

'A few minutes, Sarkar. I will find him.'

Each time the Nawab added 'Sahab' to a worker's name, it was known to be the harbinger of an extraordinary rage.

It had been a translucent morning bathed in gentle shades of daylight. The town-crier had lumbered out of the

royal gardens, in a crisp, taut pyjama and *saleem shahi* shoes – elaborate ones with snoots turned upwards. He sounded his drum to catch the ears of women with nubile daughters.

'Listen, all mothers of girls. Tomorrow, after evening prayers, keeping with the tradition of years bygone, bring your well-attired daughters to the Meena Bazaar in the Royal Gardens. You will be given transport fare.' The perfect ploy for mothers to head for a regal jaunt.

He made his way thus through tight, curling lanes; many maternal hearts were set aflutter, their gasps and shrieks were the day's background score. After all, Nawab Habib Yar Jung would pay for their entry, time and all that they picked from the bazaar's stalls. The thrill, however, came with a premium. One that desecrated the heart of a mother and yet was inescapable.

The sun went down. In the light from the crystal canopy, Noor Mahal assumed a celestial form. Habib Yar Jung took leaden steps to balance his overhanging paunch and spread himself on his wide bed, a *takht*, made of gold. His cherished scotch was placed before him in a gilded carafe by a bearer. Dark, liquid brass in cut glass beakers heightened his intoxication.

Mirza Sahab finally made an overdue entrance. 'Your slave is here, Sarkar.'

'So, what shall I do? Worship you? I did tell you this morning that an entire day's fast leaves me seething in the evening. Do you remember?'

Mirza was unable to identify his fault. Nawab Habib broke it to him. 'I told you I want to dissolve the marriages I had last year. It must happen tonight. Have you prepared the list?'

Mirza was relieved for himself, doleful for the young girls. 'Yes. It was completed this afternoon.'

'Bring it to me. I will gather them after *tarawih* prayers and carry out each divorce.'

'As you say. But...'

'That's that! Mirza!' A large gulp of alcohol softened him a little. 'But what, Mirza?'

'Some are pregnant.'

'That is why I must relieve them. I am suspicious that they aren't my children. How can I stay with dishonourable women?'

Mirza raised a doubtful brow. He was the axis of the Nawab's world. Despite the master's hysterics, he had his respect and trust, and was the only one who could offer advice. And in turn, he knew well that the loyal attendant held sway over royal pursuits of depraved intimacy.

After he returned from the mosque, a swarm of nubile beauties breezed in. Ingenuous captives, oblivious to life's wayward ways, they were rounded up like livestock. As pale and powerless as shadows, the girls fell into a line. Some had taken their first postcoital bath under this roof. Today, the grand savage looked at them with apathy. Mirza stood

holding the register and began after a signal from his master. The door would now shut firmly on the girls' fates.

The first was Ayesha Begum, aged fifteen. 'Ayesha Begum, I, Habib Yar Jung, divorce you three times and relieve you.' He handed her a paper.

'You will receive ten thousand rupees for your expenses and to raise any child you carry, although I doubt its paternity. It is a matter of integrity and status. If, in this year, there has been a slip up from me, I apologize. But I know that in this palace no hurt could have come to you. Farewell.'

Salima Begum, fourteen, Qamar Sultana, sixteen, Raisa Zamani, fifteen, Pyari Bi, thirteen, Mubarak Begum, Zehra Bibi, Fatima Begum, Suraiya, Nishat Ara... Their names kept rolling off Mirza's tongue. The same words were said to each one and divorce deeds were handed out.

Not one was over sixteen. Each face a blossoming bud, every eye heavy with a plea. They knew any dissent would crash against the customs of his palace.

Most of Hyderabad city belonged to Habib Yar Jung. His ancestors were close to the royalty and his estate was a collection of rewards for royal sycophancy. It was dotted with edifices of his elders – from mansions, *deoris* and havelis to separate wings for servants.

The Nawab's grandfather had been the lifeline of a top trader in the city. The manor was built on the merchant's

instructions, stretching from the *awami* gate all the way to the men's section and the driveway. Pathways laid with cobbled red stone and gem-studded floors. If there was an attempt to pry them out, the suspect would be lashed. All his buildings in the city were rented out to his subjects, who kept their heads bowed. Sometimes, they did glance skywards to question their imprisoned lives.

Mehtab stripped off her golden gharara and shirt. 'I am not going anywhere.'

'Tabi, if you don't, you will die before death takes you. Girls in this locality have to go to the Meena Bazaar,' said her mother.

'I know and it makes your own happiness forbidden.'

'You are so sensible, yet you say such silly things.'

'Ammi, you know I am married,' Tabi clenched her fists and screamed.

Sakina Begum sealed her daughter's mouth with a firm hand. 'Lower your voice. It mustn't reach another's ears.' Tabi forced her hand away with resolute haste. 'What if Nawab Sahab takes a shine to me? I will join his harem. How can I be a wife to two men? You are so pious, Ammi, but you have nothing to say about this? Is it so insignificant that your daughter will be a wife to two men?'

'But my child, if we don't go, will we be safe? If Nawab Sahab learns that Murad Mian's widow had the audacity to miss this occasion, we will not live to tell the tale.'

Sakina became sullen. More defenceless than her daughter, she took a seat.

Mehtab was beautiful and wilful, the toast of Kotla Alijah. She had married her cousin Tahir during the season of Urs. In the din and frenzy of ceremonies, a carriage with five men and a Qazi at their doorstep had gone unnoticed. For long, the adolescent bride had been eager to go to her husband's house. But in a neighbourhood packed with royal spies, a young girl's move was a death wish. Especially for homes where women lived on a pension from *him*. The husbands were his servants and, as their widows with few means, his stipend was sustenance for these women. Sakina was one of them.

Tahir once suggested that they flee in the dead of the night. Mehtab had trembled at the thought. The Nawab's reach frightened her; he could sneak up and sentence them to grinding wheat in his kitchens.

Sakina's recollections made her more desperate. She wanted Mehtab to dress elaborately and show up. 'Dark and modest... It is unlikely that he will notice her. I will paste her hair with oil and fulfil this formality,' she consoled herself.

The Nawab always had his silver chair placed at the entrance to cast an eye over each face and pick his harem's new delights without delay.

Fate's is a certain power. Mehtab was darker than most and drenched in oil, but the master's ardent eye went past the cloud and caught the moon. He halted Sakina Begum in her tracks and summoned them to the palace the next morning.

Tahir had arrived on a week's leave for Eid. Anguish hung over the house like a wet blanket. He was sore with misery and Sakina was an effigy of pain.

'I will kill this man,' he cried.

Sakina put her hand on his mouth. 'Son, think of the neighbours.'

'No Khala, if I don't take Tabi on the last train tonight, I am not my father's son.'

'And you forget he is waiting for her?'

'Either he lives or I do.' Tahir refused to waver.

'If you die, you think this custom will end?' asked Sakina. 'He sends his maids to keep an eye on homes where girls are close to puberty. Then he selects them in his bazaar, uses them for a year and, in the name of religion, turns them out.'

'I will not let my woman go anywhere, Khala.'

'Don't scream this way. I don't have the courage to take him on.'

Stiffened with torment, Tabi said, 'Tahir, why should you

suffer? I will kill him tonight and put an end to everyone's despair.'

'This blossoming body bruises with my kisses. It hasn't carried my child yet. My girl still hasn't learnt to harden her grip in my embrace. How can she go to that ogre? I will explain to him, and then...' He trailed off.

Eid was three days away and sleep eluded Mirza. Piles of chores filtered through his mind. From having Noor Mahal polished for festivities to clearing old wives from the haveli and ushering in new ones. Putting their shimmering wardrobes, jewels, bangles, henna, and the devine scent of *oudh* for their clothes, in order. It was strange that intricacies were given to Mirza and not to the *mughlanis*, but he was well versed in these details.

A new sun was beginning to stir. He got up to say his morning prayers and lay down when he finished. Just then, there was a knock on his door. The young visitor ran past the gateman and landed at Mirza's foyer. An irate Mirza opened his door.

'Forgive me for the inconvenience, but I know you wield influence in the Nawab's affairs. Can you take me to meet him?' asked the young man.

'Tell me the nature of your work.'

'I am a poor student and want to seek his sponsorship.'

Mirza considered the youth's request, knowing that no one was sent away empty-handed during Ramzan and that his master would not break his last fast till he'd distributed the heap of cash set on a sizable silver tray. He told the boy to wait.

'Okay, sit down. He is reciting the Quran after which he shall meet the needy. But what impact will my word have?'

'It was always my wish to get his blessings, Sahab.'

'Don't worry.' Mirza picked up a jug and went into the women's section.

Nawab Sahab took a long look at him and smiled. Tahir, being the best orator in his college, held forth without hesitation.

'I really wanted to meet a great man like you and I had no idea that such a wish could come true. Stories of your generosity and charity are narrated to our generations.'

'Boy, state what you want. It is time for my rest,' said the Nawab.

'Sarkar, I have just one request. Please leave Mehtab for me. She is my wife.'

This startled and silenced Nawab Habib. He took a long pause, then spoke. 'You know your girl has just attained

puberty. Nikah is illegal.'

'But Tabi was prepubescent when we married.'

'Mian, you have very long hands,' the Nawab remarked suggestively. 'I will let you know after I have thought about it. Please have this watch near the cloak fixed by the *gharisaz* at the watch shop. Take it with care, the chain is of real diamonds.' He handed the watch to Tahir.

Tahir was hauled across the driveway with force. Before he reached the gate, he turned to look up. The Nawab stood with Mirza on the terrace, watching the spectacle.

The Nawab then smiled at Mirza, 'Tell Amin Sahab at the police station that the poor boy must be fasting so he mustn't beat him. Confinement will be enough.'

'But swiping diamonds is hardly a small crime and that too your ancestral heirloom,' said Mirza. But the Nawab had already left.

Mehtab refused to sign the nikah papers and the Nawab didn't subscribe to force in matters of religion.

'I cannot resist this girl. Take her out, pamper her, show her my riches so that she agrees to be with me.'

'But she also said that she was married. You know that another nikah is illegal,' Mirza reasoned, citing holy verses.

'I think it's a trap. Wait for the right time.'

The next day, all his bequests to Tabi went to waste. She hurled his lavish dishes out of her house; the grand clothes that she was presented with were ripped to pieces and she sat naked.

'Naked?' The Nawab rolled his tongue across his lips when he heard of her reaction. He thought of his fast and contained his thrill. 'Doesn't matter. It has happened before. Time takes care of everything.'

The Eid moon rose, announcements echoed through the city and Noor Mahal glowed like a lucent stone.

Mirza rushed in with clasped hands. 'That watch thief, Sarkar... He died.'

'Died? So delicate that he couldn't withstand four lashes?'

'No, he dislodged the bars of the top window and was trying to climb out when he fell. The window was too high, so he died.'

The Nawab lay down. 'That's not our fault.'

'Not at all. I just came to inform you. If he really was Mehtab Begum's husband, then she is a widow now.'

In the morning, as Nawab Sahab mounted his carriage to leave for Eid prayers, a distressed Mirza scampered in.

'There has been a calamity. Mehtab died too.'

'What? How?'

'She powdered her glass bangles and swallowed them.'

Habib Yar Jung sat in his carriage and cupped his hands towards the sky. 'Me, an insignificant creature, how can I thank you, my Lord. You protected me from sin. I could have had blood on my hands.'

'Don't they know suicide is forbidden?' he said to Mirza.

A servant held the traditional tray, stacked with gold coins. The Nawab believed that prayer was not accepted until these were handed out.

He put his hand on the coins, the coachman cracked his whip. Amid songs of peace and blessings from his aides, he set out for the mosque.

4

Rozi Ka Sawaal

The Cost of Survival

Ashraf, not livelier than a plantlet, was living a bad dream in this orbit of sex. Shalu spread a sheer pallu on her bare breasts and sprang to face him, crackling with rage.

'You bloody storyteller, don't call me Bibi! Don't you dare insult me. Bibi, the sister you sleep with! For you, a pen moves on paper. Here, hands move on our bodies. Either write like that or I will kick you to the stairs.'

Her more voluptuous rival swooped on the opportunity to trap a client. 'O bloody keep of your husband! He was walking towards me.'

'Ah, so you could sleep in his lap. Daddy, isn't he?'

'Of course, or was he your son? Come for your milk, had he?'

'I'll rip your mouth down to your stomach, horsy slut!'

As they leapt at each other like two fire saltines collide, Ashraf cursed the moment the idea of setting down their stories had come to him. He stood deadened by their obscenities and the stormy scenes before him. Shalu clenched the other woman's hair and shreds of her rival's blouse swayed in her flailing hands.

Struck by a streak of reason, the breathless contender pleaded, 'Wait, let's ask him who he wants to go to.'

Shalu vaulted to her feet and caught Ashraf by the collar. Her warm breath against his skin. 'Say. Who did you want? You want me.' She was wild. An unnerved Ashraf sputtered in panic. 'Uh, yes...yes...I...ah I...me...'

'You sound like a little lost goat. She is a bitch. Now say you came for Shalu.'

Words froze on his tongue as he turned to her and then to the other.

'Should I slap you to say it?'

Ashraf, at long last, knew where survival lay. 'Yes, yes, I am here to meet you.'

'Meet? O Sahab. You "meet" your mothers and sisters. Do we look like them?' she sneered.

'Yes...yes...you see I want to write an experimental film.'

'Filum,' Shalu repeated, smug in the belief of having caught on to his plan. 'You are here to recruit extras, I see.'

'Extra?' Ashraf murmured, then came alive with a wry

smile. 'No, you are wrong. Not extras. I am a writer and came in search of a tale.'

Disappointed, Shalu grew testy. 'Sahab, put it this way, your car is running on empty.' He turned to peer down at the lane below. None of the cars was his and neither would one be for a long time to come. 'See, Shalu, I don't own a car so the question of petrol does not arise.'

'You fool! You don't know the meaning of the phrase? A limp man, in our parlance, is a car without petrol. Did you catch that, you Writer Sahab?'

Her detail gave him the shakes; he began to turn into a pool of brine. If she were a man it would be a different story, he thought. Chunni, once again, sensed the brittleness of the moment and moved away. 'Ha!' she thumbed her nose. 'You play this punctured drum, I am leaving.'

'You bitch! Why did you say that about my customer?'

'What else? I shall say it a hundred times! Deflated drum!' What can you do?

'Did I give him a signal? You whore! It's you who let your pallu slip!'

Ashraf's mission had only served to heighten Chunni's conceit. 'I let my pallu fall? You are so jealous of my bosom, with your insect-bite knots. The pallu can't cope with me.'

'I know your secret. I don't stuff rubber in my blouse,' Shalu snarled.

'What! What did you say? I keep rubber. Here, see for

yourself.' In a single sweep, Chunni ripped off her blouse. Ashraf looked up, now stiff with the petrol this world lived on. But he turned his back with a faint refrain. 'Shalu, you start such trivial fights.'

A stern voice wafted out of a nearby room. 'Chunni, how much longer does your customer have to wait? What are you doing? It's the milkman!'

'Go, cow. It is your brother, go get milked!'

Chunni's was a proud retort. 'See, he too has come for me.'

Shalu shot back with cold reason. 'He is a fixed customer, I understand that. But if it is a walk-in and you leap out of turn, will I not react? Isn't this my livelihood too?'

The voice had come into view now. Decaying black teeth, the contours of her mouth stained with betel juice, a half-burnt roll-up stuck behind her ear, dark, plump face with burgundy lips – she was Chunni's madame, in a floral sari.

'Sahab, salaam for Baiji?' Chunni said to Ashraf. But before he could catch up with etiquette, Shalu had a score to settle. 'You will never know English. I have told you to call her Mummy. Oye Sahab, in the entire *chawl* I am the only one familiar with English. You know why? I was in a movie.'

He did not want to spark another clash, so he swallowed the wisecrack that was on the tip of his tongue. 'Oh, was it ever released?'

'No, Sahab, and I am responsible for that debacle.'

'How?'

'An extra supplier took five of us to...what do you call a filmmaker?'

'Director.'

'Whatever. Sounds like some relative of a doctor... anyway, he asked me to recite a *diaalok* in a certain way.'

'Diaalok?' Ashraf repeated. 'You mean dialogue?'

'I told you. No one else here knows English. Stop interrupting, it disturbs me,'

'Sorry... I will be quiet.'

'Why will you be quiet? You know what a *mukka* is? Someone who can't talk. Don't treat me as if I were a talking parrot. You can speak but only when you can't understand an English word!'

Amused and calm, Ashraf agreed. 'Correct.'

'So I was saying, that filmmaker told me to say the line without looking at him or he would punch me in the eye. And the villain, you understand "villain"?'

'Yes, I do. Then?'

'So, the villain glared at me with bloodshot eyes. I ran towards him, screaming, "If you look at me, I will punch your eye." But my fist missed his eye. Everyone scrambled around him, instead of clapping for me. He fell to the floor with blood on his face.'

Ashraf cupped his cheek to cover a smile. 'Yes, your talent was past that director's grasp.'

'Oh, I didn't get into all that. You know why?'

'No.'

'I understood that, you know, the business we do in our rooms here happens in the open with extras. You tell me, is this better or that kind of shameless fame?'

His mind had wandered to when Baiji took Chunni's hand and disappeared behind their hovel.

Chunni, fixing her pallu and blouse, finally emerged from the nook and balked, 'You're still babbling and I have tended to a customer.'

'How much?' Shalu asked with enthusiasm.

'The same fixed for every day, three rupees.'

The grief that flashed across Shalu's face did not escape Ashraf. 'Just once?' she asked Chunni in their code, alien to him.

'Then how many times? Diwali and Eid are so close. Look at the crowds. Customers come in droves and we have to service quickly.' And they burst into giggles. Their fights and camaraderie eluded this benign man. He tried to leave numerous times, but the artist's quest in him, and Shalu's arm hooked around his elbow, kept him glued.

Moments later, the two girls spotted a shy man, afraid to be an open customer as he peered meekly through the bars of their tight prison cell of a hovel.

'Come, get up to some mischief with me,' Chunni let her pallu slip to flaunt her prized chest.

'Oh, please don't repeat this trick,' Ashraf appealed, afraid of another pang of desire. Shalu was chuffed with her steady catch. 'Look, I told you. This is my customer. He has only looked at me.'

'As if you have any stamina! Your tongue wagging isn't enough; wag a lot else to trap a real customer.'

'I do twelve customers in a night. Who do you think I am?'

'I just see a pubescent waist.'

'Listen, you busty, fat whore! Men love my body. They stay in me and hold me. I am not a well of poison like you. As soon as a man finishes with you, he rushes out to wash himself.' Before Chunni could respond, Baiji entered carrying bhelpuri in a soiled saucer.

'Shalu, you are greedy. Chunni gave me eight paise extra for bhelpuri and her commission.'

'And a sari on Diwali, earrings for Eid...'

Shalu looked away, towards the loitering, bashful boy in the distance. Baiji took a large dollop of her spicy chutney, then spoke to Ashraf gruffly. 'Now what?'

'What do you mean by now? There was nothing between us earlier.'

'I know, that is why I asked.'

A sudden realization of having been out of line loomed over him. In the dying sun, at their prime business hour, he was a dent in their pockets. 'I will pay more than you expect, I promise,' he said.

She let out a cackle. 'You will pay fifty rupees for chatter? Even those who come to pass time pay at least twenty-five rupees.'

'I will take another hour or two and give you a hundred rupees,' he offered with urgency. Baiji gaped and her plate fell to the floor. In a flash, Shalu and Chunni were wrapped around him.

'Sahab, who will you give this money to?'

'Sahab, is it for me?'

'No, Sahab, speak the truth. You smiled at me first.'

'Don't be shy. You winked at me.'

Ashraf's head spun. He yearned to revile the dimwit who gave him the idea of writing on prostitutes to earn a name.

Shalu was sharper. 'Look, Chunni, that boy at the window has his eye on you.' As Chunni went behind the curtain to freshen up, Shalu bent over Ashraf's shoulder. 'There goes the whore. Now you do whatever you like, but the money is mine.'

Ashraf, like a fool, asked, 'But where did Chunni go?'

'To the back for the boy at the window.'

'Why did you let her go?'

She moved away in anguish. 'Are you really such an oaf? He can't cough up more than five rupees and that's why I told her he wanted her. Now I have you and your hundred rupees.'

'But I am giving 100 for your time.'

'Yes, Sahab, I know. But that horrid old whore will take forty and that pimp another ten, so that leaves fifty for me.'

'This mummy and the pimp, what is the story there?'

'Sahab, are you really so oblivious about us? Baiji has ten or twelve girls and has a man who sweet talks customers like you to come to us. So, half of our earning goes to these two.'

'Do you call him *bharwa* then?'

She was nonchalant. 'Anyone can call him whatever they want. We say what is convenient. But we have to call this old slut "mummy" and "witch" behind her back. The pimp, *bharwa*, is *khoitia*. If we bring a catch on our own, that is "catching a pigeon". If he ropes someone in, then it's "catching a rooster". A client who stays for an all-nighter is *baithna* and for sex we say "how many were painted with henna".'

Ashraf melted slowly in dismay as Shalu kept at it.

'These are trade secrets, we don't tell everyone, Sahab. Since you say you write stories, I am telling you all this in the hope that perhaps one day you will write of our fate. I am the only one who speaks English. The rest just spread themselves on various beds. I read the paper too but not with this money...with lice money.'

'Lice money?' He was now unsteady with shock.

'Yes, madame is always intoxicated. Sometimes she has her legs pressed, back massaged, lice picked. For legs, she pays fifty rupees for an hour, and five annas per louse. So, I

keep *kala zeera* tied in my pallu, and drop ten to twenty seeds in her hair and then pluck them out to put in her palm.'

'Would you like to tell me why you have this love of earning money by conning people? First you beat up Chunni, then send her off with Baiji and now that you know I will pay a hundred, you have fooled her into serving that boy. What is all this?'

'The cost of survival, Sahab,' she replied softly.

'But it is the same for Chunni and all the others I have not seen. They must be in these cages too.'

'Ah, don't get all worked up. All dance to their own tunes.'

'Then tell me, how much have you collected so far?'

Shalu looked around to ensure her secret was safe and whispered, 'One thousand, five hundred.' She expected a dazzled reaction. He may not have been a writer of renown, but he did manage some twenty thousand rupees. He schooled his face to protect her pride and asked, 'What will you do with so much money?'

'I will have my own house.'

In that moment, a story had taken form before him, complete with her sobering reply.

Three years later, Ashraf's movie on prostitutes set the box office afire. His rise to stardom, riches, and the fanfare that followed was almost fictional. Yet, Shalu was his first thought. He followed his heart in a swanky car to her squalid lane. Stale faces, dark skins grey with talcum powder and

crimson lips jeered from their cages. He climbed up to Shalu's room. Baiji, a cigarette behind her ear, munched on bhelpuri from the same soiled saucer.

She stumbled at the sight of his car, but assumed he wasn't worthy of it and returned to her snack. A towering man stood before her. She was baffled by Ashraf's new, polished avatar. Baiji's composure was transient, she hobbled and her saucer came crashing down. Four girls scattered around the room, giggled.

'Where is Shalu Bibi?'

'Why do you ask for old, stale flesh? Come. Look at them!' She stretched her arm out towards the nubile flock.

'I want to talk to Shalu. She will have some more money to build a house.'

'House?' Baiji gasped.

'And Chunni?'

'Chunni? She rotted.'

'What?'

'Yes. Her torso was covered in warts and everyone was too afraid to even give her water. Shalu took her to the hospital. God! I spent so much money on her illness.'

'Really? But I remember the two fighting so mercilessly.' Ashraf was as disoriented as he was when he had first come here.

'Shalu said that it is a matter of Chunni's livelihood and no one will touch her in this state. Then she took her.'

'Do you know which hospital?'

'Sahab, she caught the ailment from Chunni and became far too frail. I didn't go to them nor were my girls allowed to see them. If others caught it, what would happen to my earning?'

Ashraf, however numb, forced himself to manage a silent departure. For him, Shalu was now cleansed of all misgivings. Her words and memory ran as vividly through his mind as his own film.

She had said to him, 'Sahab, you know those four walls should belong to me. No one expects marriage. But a prostitute's old age is the toughest. I have seen them perish on footpaths. I must have a house where I plant flowers and the breeze wafts through my hair.'

Ashraf wanted to call out her name with all his strength. But he could not find his voice. It was lost, like so much within him. He had all of two hundred rupees at the time. Gathering his own fragments, he quietly put the money in the old woman's palm and slowly walked away, almost in dread of his days to come.

5

Talaq, Talaq, Talaq

Separation

She held back the scream of dread from escaping her. She was too feisty to surrender, too pragmatic to fear his death. Nawab Sarkar had a gun on Sher Khan's chest. His heart as restless as a captive moth, cascades of sweat ran down Sher's temples to his neck. Nervous and desolate, he felt as though he was in a state of suspension – *barzakh* – between heaven and earth.

'Say talaq three times, Khan!'

'Sarkar, don't commit this cruelty. Mehru is my life, my world.'

'Just say it and save your life. You'll find many fine women,' rang Mehru's cold, loud advice from the balcony of

their room. Then she turned to scan her beloved husband's Sarkar.

'This is my final order. Say the words or take a bullet. I have run out of patience. Come on, say it. I, Jamal Khan, give talaq to my wife, Mehru. Three times.'

A defeated whimper came from his strapping, solid body. 'I, Jamal Khan, give my wife, Mehru, talaq, talaq, talaq.

'Bless your woman. She saved you or you would have been a corpse.' The Nawab put his gun aside.

'Now remember these words, Nawab Sahab,' quipped Mehru. A deep love of so many years was so fragile when hostage to three little words, she thought on her way out of their quarter with the aristocrat.

Jamal slid down to the floor, his wet, sullen face between his knees. He saw a vacant forever unfold before him. 'Where do I go now!' he thought, languid with wild despair.

In the opulent haveli, Sher's newly former wife tried a bargain. 'No, Sahab. Don't send him so far. You know he saved your life. Let him be put to work in your haveli.'

'Why? You think my lands are so barren that they can't feed a lone man?' the Nawab's tone was nurturing.

'Lands?' Mehru's delirium stayed hidden by the cover of his infatuation.

A few miles from Hyderabad Deccan lay Mausam, the Nawab's verdant village, where he often slid into the past. His first visit was as a child with his father. The poetic landscape of the place had captivated him.

'Abba Jaan, each season is aroused to its fullest here. What an apt name for our village!' the Nawab recalled their conversations. 'Yes son, we also have the finest shikar here.'

The son then went on a rampage, bringing home nilgai, deer, tigers. The proud father would have him pose in breeches with each carcass, one foot resting on the animal, chest thrust forward. These were plastered on the walls with ensuing pageantry.

The grand pashas decided it was time for wedding bells to toll in their mansion. A well-heeled home with three daughters was found and the eldest was chosen to become his bride. A porcelain young woman, as fresh as dew, had him hypnotized at first sight. A son was born in their first year together, with another two in the years that followed. The Nawab had no interest in hunting expeditions anymore. The thrill of the bullet had been replaced.

'Whoever imagined that there were pleasures greater than the triumphs of a hunt?' he would often muse aloud. 'What can I say. The shackles on me are as dense and alluring as her dark, scented hair that spreads all over me.'

At home, his Dulhan, raised in the cradle of luxury and

honour, saw his maddened love as her birthright and Nawab Salim soon became a novelty in his surroundings as a rare, if not lone, slave to conjugal love.

That day at his ancestral hamlet, the news of a tiger on the prowl had jolted him out of his trance. Once every three or four days, it came here to hunt. Old fears of villagers falling prey to the tiger plagued the townlet. For the Nawab and his staff, such a mishap spelt mass exodus and wasted crops. Nawab took his gun and went to rescue his assets. As he went deep into the forest with thoughts of constructing a secure, high *machan*, he heard a stealthy rustle. A sublime tiger bounced out of the dark to confront him. This was the moment when Jamal Khan pounced with the speed of a bloodhound to attack it with an axe. His loyal servant and the beast were entangled in a savage fight. The Nawab's bravado dissipated and he fainted.

'Wake up, Sarkar. The tiger is dead. Jamal hacked it to death and saved you.' As the news flowed into his ears, his eyes opened with the wonder of a newborn. 'Jamal Khan, ask me for anything.'

A shy smile played on Jamal's lips. 'Sarkar, you have been saved. There is no greater privilege for me. My hands rescued you from its teeth.'

'You must tell me. I owe it to you.'

'You called me Sher Khan. The title is enough for me.'

This hour of vigour and gratitude was fated to take an

ominous turn. Villagers carried Jamal on their shoulders and Nawab Sahab too was exalted in the garb of a groom. A jubilant crowd swelled in numbers. Their procession halted at Jamal's house, a small hut of baked bricks. A girl, as luminous as moonlight, ran out to hold him.

She wept, as her grip tightened. 'I would have died. Did you get hurt?'

'Be careful. If his wounds fill up with water, it can be dangerous. Let the herbalist see him,' said a man in the crowd.

'Is the herbalist his wife? He needs my touch, my clothes are his balm.' She wrapped herself around him more fiercely.

When people dispersed, the Nawab got a full view of her. She was an ode to womanhood that quickened his senses. He could picture their firestorms at nightfall and decided to bring the couple to his haveli in Hyderabad.

Nawab knew that life from here on called for wisdom and a meticulous game of patience. He had to tread with care to assuage his wife, Sher Khan and the plucky Mehru. So, he sent Mehru to the women's section to serve his Begum. Mehru's attention to her needs and fuss over her baby was endearing to Dulhan Begum. 'Oh Dulhan Pasha, don't take a bath in this cold,' said Mehru on chilly evenings.

Before she left for her quarter at night, she placed quilts by Dulhan's feet and with a flattering giggle, she'd say, 'If you ask me, there will be no need for them. You will be warm in other ways.'

One day, worried for the royal heir, she offered, 'Pasha, the cleric's beard will frighten our precious little Nawab. I can teach him.'

'So you can read and write?' asked the Begum, happy to learn of her skills.

'Yes, I completed nine classes, then my father chose Jamal Khan and got me married. I lived in Hyderabad, went to school here, learnt Urdu and mathematics in a *madressah*, and *namaz* too.'

'But I never see you pray?'

'Where's the time, Pasha? When I return to my quarter, my husband and I make wild love. You know after long hours of separation, every pore is on fire. How many times can I bathe for prayers? God will forgive me. I do say my sunrise prayers, even if it's a little late.'

Although the hunger between the Nawab and his Begum was known in Hyderabad, he still bragged about their amorous exploits and his indifference to temptation with the loud zeal of a fishmonger. The Dulhan Begum wanted to compete with Mehru and Jamal's lustful excesses.

'Nawab is like that too. So many years have gone by, but his passion is ceaseless. Just like your man, even when I was pregnant with the boys, he wanted his loins quenched.'

As Nawab Salim watched the two women, he felt a strange sense of solace. This was chess, his moves were artful. He pretended to be irked by their familiarity.

'Is it necessary? They're below the ground you walk on, Begum. You're from beyond the stars,' would be his gripe. But, in his mind, like a wanton wraith, the truth was ever present. 'I have Mehru lodged in my groin, my wildest fantasy.'

In this sprawling haveli, the *durbans* blew trumpets to convey messages and signals to other sections. Sher Khan was stationed in the *deori* of the male wing, with little to occupy him. He was summoned often to the Nawab's chambers where his story of valour was shared with the town's elite.

'This is the boy who saved the Nawab. He killed a tiger with his axe,' they would say as he walked past.

Nawabs carried their hearts in their palms, their palms in their pockets and their ploys close to their chests. Jamal enjoyed a rupee or two every day and sometimes even a gold coin. His ferocity had to be dulled.

'You're a nawab now,' Mehru would playfully say.

'When was I not? I always had you, my statuette of gold. Show me a royal in Hyderabad who can match that. I have the kind of love that if I were to die tomorrow, I would not go with sadness. God gave you to me as my fortune.'

It took some months, but Nawab Salim's long wait and stealthy moves culminated in a fashion similar to the

fateful night of his assault. This had been the only time in Mehru's life when she did not call out to her God or cry in distress. Instead, she had facilitated her split from Jamal. 'See Pasha, he is so useful. He saved you,' were her words that broke Jamal. The shock of his darling converting into a conspirator had castrated him. 'She always spoke of God as if he were her own, and today she didn't remember Him. As my wife, she will never know the riches that come with being this rich bastard's mistress!'

After Mehru told him to divorce her and walked out of their marriage, Jamal was confined to the outhouse at the back of the estate and Mehru's was a deluxe boudoir between the two wings. A woman's instincts led her to the innermost recesses of a man's heart. Therefore, she always knew that the Nawab's surface belied his true self. His stolen visit to her room was no surprise.

'Remember, if you ever told Dulhan Pasha that I got you a divorce and came to your room, no one will believe you. Our love is so well known.' He settled on her bed expectantly and continued, 'Your bond is severed now. To marry you, I had to get you divorced. But we will marry later, in secrecy. I am a man. I know the rage a man has towards the woman he divorces. It makes him a reptile and I am sure Sher Khan has become that now.'

Spears flew from her eyes as she looked up, but she chose silence. She began to play with her lips, indifferent to his

confessions and desire. 'If divorce was so necessary then follow the other conditions in religion too.'

'You mean?'

'I have to complete my days of seclusion after divorce.'

'You idiot.' He caught her hand. She flung it off. 'Don't touch me. I have my period.'

He made feeble attempts to flirt, then got up to leave with a laconic warning. 'If you meet Sher Khan, remember it is a sin.'

'Oh yes! This is so pure,' she stung.

A week later, Mehru took the ceremonial cleansing bath after menstruation, glistening like finely cut glass. 'Don't look so irresistible or my husband will have eyes for you,' teased Dulhan Begum.

Mehru was icy. 'He already does.'

Unable to stand her audacity, the incensed Begum breathed fire. 'Are you in your senses, you slut!'

'*Nawabzadi*, I have enough sense. Now listen to me. Nawab Salim wants me between his thighs. Come to my room tonight, lie on my bed in the dark, see the truth unravel.'

Her mansion felt as silent as a grave and then, after a pause, she, smelling deceit, asked, 'Why?'

'He will come for me tonight. My period week ended today.'

Dulhan still nursed some hope. 'And if he doesn't?'

'Cut my hair, have me beaten and thrown on the streets.'

In the night, Mehru sparkled like a bride and went to see her husband. Jamal sat on the floor, staring blankly into the dark.

'Today I want a spectacle. Come to my room, Jamal.'

'And Nawab?'

She took him to the boundary wall and told him to stay till she called out. 'Come on. Lead the way to our freedom. I can sell fifteen such nawabs in one paisa.'

As the night quietened, the Nawab took careful, measured steps towards Mehru's room. A tame knock and the door was pushed open. In the dim light of the oil lamp, Dulhan was an outline of a slender mirage on Mehru's bed. Salim slid closer, Dulhan Pasha turned the lamp brighter. For a few minutes her fury froze in the air, they stared at each other in horror. 'Hum, hum...' he stammered.

Dulhan leapt to her feet. 'Don't you know Urdu? *Hum* is two. You are alone. Now say, I give my wife, Gulbadan Bibi, a divorce. Say it three times or I'll call my father. Don't you ever think that I fed off the crumbs of your table. Nawabs like you live in my father's hand-me-downs.'

Mehru entered from the back room. 'Oh! you're here? How are both of you in my hovel?'

'Go and call your husband,' Begum said tenderly. She went out, called Jamal who was by the wall, and the two walked in together. Begum asked Mehru to spread her wrap, then peeled off every particle of gold on her body and placed

it on the shawl. 'You opened my eyes, my girl. Jamal, you are so lucky. Such a picture of love and loyalty isn't common. I vouch that when she carries a child, it will be yours.'

Salim watched with eyes that could bore a hole in the mortar. Having accomplished her cold revenge, Mehru walked out holding Jamal's hand.

'That's my hand.'

'So, what happened to it?'

'We are divorced. Don't you know what a woman must do to return to her husband?'

'I would slaughter the man I have to get a divorce from to come to you. Where is your pride? I just saved myself from a brute and should go to another? In my religion, if you are dying of hunger, even pork is allowed.'

'Yes, I know. But...'

'In helplessness the forbidden is permitted, Jamal.'

'Yes.'

'He forced you to divorce me. How is that legal? If it happens at gunpoint, it's unacceptable to God. Wait, I just remembered something.'

Not one to be placated easily, she pulled him into a room where Nawab Salim sat, head in his hands like a forsaken gambler turning to dust, and launched into a venomous tirade.

'Nawab, I always despised Noor Jahan for a reason. She was Sher Afghan's widow, who shed a few tears at his death

and moved on with Emperor Jahangir to rule Hindustan. They were Salim and Mehr-un-nisa. You are Salim and I am Mehru. You named my husband, the man who saved you, Sher Khan. What did you think? That I would weep, then surrender to your loins just like Mehr-un-nisa did to Salim? A man who can make me turn away from my husband is not in this world.'

The defeated Sarkar looked up in silent shame and disbelief.

Mehru and Jamal walked away hand in hand. Jamal, who choked up with guilt at having suspected Mehru of desire and avarice, smiled to himself. 'True, my wife is pure, but rather quick-tempered...'

Moments later, his remorse was doused in a blaze of delight.

Pride

1

Lungi Kurta

The Exchange

Shabnam and Arshad Mian were a natural match; she was beautiful and he a model of masculinity. Furthermore, Arshad Mian had not one but ten virtues that made him an exception among his peers. His loyalty was one of them.

So, when his proposal was sent for Shabbo, there was not the slightest chance of it being turned down. Shabbo, with the help of her friends, caught a glimpse of her groom-to-be; it had made her dizzy with delight.

Not long ago, two of her friends had tied the knot, but they were hesitant about introducing their husbands to other friends. She knew this was not her fate; her consort was handsome and affluent, with several servants to tend to

his kitchen. He also had his own car and two others for the rest of his family.

Shabnam was elated. Their wedding night was right out of her dreams. The bridal room was opulent, like a movie set, and her groom's words fell like nectar on her ears.

'Shabnam, like your name, you fell like dew on my heart. I can't believe that a heavenly being is in my arms, that I can touch and feel you. You're not a dream. I'm so happy that we found each other,' he said.

In any other scenario, Shabnam would have laughed. In this moment, she felt beautiful, loved and fortunate.

'Someone who has you, needs nothing else.'

She studied him from the corner of her eye, looked over his perfect contours, fleshy lips that moved in her praise, and a sudden sensation of heat and wetness took over all coyness.

She freshened up on the first morning of her new life in her new home and blushed as her mother-in-law entered.

'Did my son tease you too much last night?' she joked and Shabnam froze with embarrassment.

'Listen, dear, we have a certain rule in our house. The dress worn for the wedding is not worn again. It must be given away to an unmarried girl as a blessing from the bride.'

Shabnam was dejected. Her dress held immortal memories for her, not just for its delicacy but also for her first moments of rapture with her husband. However, she

had to abide by the rules of the house. She consoled herself with the thought that she had enough money to buy ten such dresses. But there was more to come from the matriarch.

'You must have changed into nightwear after taking it off – that too has to be donated to someone.' She spoke without sentiment or empathy.

Shabnam listened with her head lowered. A day-old bride could hardly counter her husband's mother. The moment her mother-in-law left, Arshad Mian entered and said, 'Listen, Shabbo, you can give the wedding dress and nightdress to any of my sisters. Just don't give any clothes to the maids.'

He saw her questioning eyes. 'I have this fear. I have also told my mother that she must not give her clothes to the maids. Once she gave her sari to an old maid. When I returned from work, the maid was in that sari with her face turned away. Thinking it was my mother, I hugged her. I was ridden with shock and embarrassment. I can give new clothes to our staff but I cannot allow them to wear our old clothes.' He was as adamant as his mother.

Shabnam looked on in awe as he continued, 'And, especially now, I wouldn't want any maid in my wife's clothes. I cannot imagine it. Please, my dear, don't be hurt.'

Shabnam burst into a laugh.

'Don't laugh. I'm serious, I cannot see anyone else in your clothes.'

'Okay, I will keep that in mind,' she assured him softly.

But Shabnam could not keep her promise for long. There was a legion of servants and maids in the house. There was Karmu, a twenty-five-year-old man, well-built and the colour of wheat. He looked after Arshad Mian, ever ready for any task that came his way. Gulbadan catered to Shabnam. She was as removed from her name, which meant a body made of flowers, as one could imagine – plump and without the faintest trace of charm.

Shabnam was amused by Gulbadan's name. *Badan* – a word that promised sensuousness, romance and a certain mischief – in this instance belonged to one who could frighten people in the moonlight and would be hard to find in the dark. Shabbo was fascinated by the similarity in the colour of Shabnam's hair and skin. She did have long, thick hair, though. When she wore a pale sari after a shower, her damp hair fell all over her back. The thought of what would follow if she gave her clothes to Gulbadan made Shabbo chuckle. She couldn't imagine her husband confusing Gulbadan for her. Even though six yards of a sari can wrap around a body of any size, the blouses would be too tight on her.

Little did she know that a man's indiscretion often began with conventionally uninviting women. They rarely had the courage to lure attractive girls because their confidence was their shield, whereas a woman unhappy with her lack of

appeal was easy prey. Arshad was as gallant as he was virile. A marital bed hot with endless lovemaking had carried his desire to a new level. Now, a slight tease could chart a reckless path.

Eventually, Shabbo forgot that her husband had forbidden her from giving her clothes to anyone in the household. She had sparkled the three times she'd worn the sari. It roused her husband whenever he saw her don the striped piece. She teased him about discarding his favourite sari and the idea had irked him.

Later that week, Gulbadan came to her and warily asked her for clothes to wear to her nephew's wedding.

'I don't have old saris, Gulbadan. I left all my old clothes at my parents' house,' she told the maid.

'Dulhan, please see. You must have something you can give me,' she pleaded.

This was the first time that a maid had asked Shabnam for something in her husband's home. She could not refuse. She saw the sari on the dresser and asked Gulbadan to take it.

'It hasn't been washed yet so still looks new. You can wear it to the wedding.'

Gulbadan had put that sari against herself several times before and admired her reflection in the mirror. Now it was hers. An overjoyed Gulbadan praised and thanked Shabbo.

That night, as Arshad Mian went to the bathroom with his

green lungi and silk kurta slung over his shoulder, Shabbo said,'You know, when I wasn't married, I disliked the lungi and kurta. Now, after marriage, I love seeing you in them.'

Arshad Mian looked at her indulgently. 'Let me change and come back.'

He came out of the bathroom, lay down by her side and held her. 'Oh, this is so sweet,' she whispered.

They had a spacious bathroom, without a lock. Initially, Shabbo was uncomfortable with this system. Then Arshad explained to her that every room in the house had its own bathroom so she could lock the room and use it in peace. 'And when I'm in the room, there is no need to lock it anyway.'

Shabbo always locked the bedroom door before she went to the bathroom. One day, when she returned from her mother-in-law's room, she set about looking for a lipstick that she couldn't find on her dressing table. Eventually, she thought of searching for it in the bathroom. Shabbo opened the bathroom door and her spine stiffened with fury, her eyes felt like burning embers, her blood congealed. The scene made her skin crawl; it was sickening enough to cling like a rotten limpet to the rest of her life with her husband. Words stuck in her throat, she slammed the door shut. But Arshad Mian saw her. He came out expecting a storm of rage, a hysterical Shabnam calling his family and stripping him of all dignity. But she was cold and quiet. He pledged innocence and implored her to forgive him. Then, he reminded her of

their first morning, when she promised him that she would not give her clothes to a maid. His words collided with her silence. She was still and soundless.

Although she wanted to break everything in sight, Shabnam knew that a fight would ease the burden of his guilt. She held on to her violent passions like fractures in a piece of crystal – no conversation, no conflict and no more promises. She watched his antics and when he grew tired of pleading his case, she called Karmu into the room.

As the strapping young man walked in, she got up from the bed and pulled out her husband's green lungi and silk kurta from the closet.

'All your clothes are torn, so this lungi and kurta are for you.'

2

Paish Bandi

In Loveless Anticipation

The mansion was brimming with flurried activity and a babel of happy voices. Maids with silver and crystal trays charged through the labyrinth of hallways. Although stirred by his imminent marriage, the thought of the *paish bandi* brought Nawab Mumtaz to a state of ecstasy. He was known to want more. Grooms who looked only to their brides and practised deference for their *paish bandi* were a rare breed and faced incessant ridicule about their manhood.

Paish bandi – having another woman accompany the new Begum as her lifelong maid – became a reason young, wealthy scions looked forward to getting married. The tradition's origins lay buried in ancient folklore. It was said that there was once a Nawab's daughter who bore the curse

of spinsterhood. She was educated but shorn of physical charm. One day, a family came to see her for their son. Fearing another rejection, her mother presented a beautiful girl in her place and the union was sealed in an instant. The ceremonies of *arsee musaf* and *jalwa numai*, where the groom saw his bride for the first time, cast a shadow of fear on her parents. A sympathetic friend came up with a way out. The bride, dressed in red brocade, was directed to faint when preparations began for their first glance and was taken to her room. The shy but excited groom, ready with a rhapsody of praise for her exquisiteness, entered the room gingerly. At first, he was confused at seeing the maid, but she quickly lured him in with her smile. Her poor parents had received a handsome reward for their daughter's services. He ran to her like a famished beast to meat. The next morning, he was awoken by his parents' cries of being deceived. 'This was my fate and I am content,' he consoled them. And so, *paish bandi* became a part of regal dowry.

At Mumtaz's palace, pageantry began on the first day of the bride's *mayyun*. Girls from her family entered the rose-pink mansion with prized baskets, delicacies, jewellery and costumes for the groom. Satin and fine silk kurtas with chamois pyjamas, Hyderabadi caps and several sherwanis. The jewels, the pearl necklace worth a hillock of gems, were declarations of their grandeur. Mumtaz's sherwani was studded with pearls. The series of rituals harked back to the era of Nawab Qadir Yar Jung's ancestors.

'Girls, prepare the water for our groom's bath!' ordered Mama Jani.

At long last, Nawab Mumtaz's anticipation would end. When a groom sat for his *mayyun*, he was covered with fragrant sandalwood paste by the sisters, cousins, friends and maids of the bride. As he lay stretched out across the *takht*, the young Nawab could feel their soft hands all over him, sending tremors down his spine.

Whenever the conviviality of a wedding breezed through the estate, all the boys began to vie for the loveliest girl in attendance.

Suddenly, a bevy of girls raced towards Mumtaz, and pulled him to the place of his shower which was supposed to be under the open sky. Four married ladies held a vibrant silk canopy over him and the fifth poured milk slowly on his head. From here, the girls took over.

'Mumtaz Bhai, after the bath, we will take *naik* from Mama Jani.'

'Sigh! It's sad that one gets to marry just once,' he thought as their fingers tickled him. He was wet between his thighs.

'Move on, Gulchaman, don't tickle! Can't you see he is uncomfortable?' the one showering rose and marigold petals on him said with a laugh.

Nawab Mumtaz turned to watch the scenes behind him. Dainty hands moved from his shoulders, down his back, all the way to his feet, lathering him in the creamy deep

yellow paste. Gulchaman, the petite girl in a kurta chosen to come with the bride, was a chiselled statuette of marble. She rubbed his back and began washing his feet, her raven hair swung by the sides of her cheeks and he felt her breasts against him. Immersed in a sensuous spell, he surrendered every pore to her touch.

'Gulchaman, where are you? Your little one is crying,' someone called out to her, jolting him out of his stupor. The idea of a woman experienced in the rites of lust, like ripened fruit being juicier than its sour youth, further kindled the Nawab's appetite.

The marriage was five days away. It would be a restless period for Mumtaz. His bride was a glass doll, but flashes of her *paish bandi*'s form, her smile and opalescent skin, swirled within him. As desire overcame him, wedding traditions became tiresome. Nawab Mumtaz wanted to toss away his turban, in fact, every piece of clothing on his body, and whisk Gulchaman off to a secluded corner.

'I want to ask you to ensure no one peeps into our room, or I will smash his head in the morning,' he told his sister-in-law as the marriage rites ended.

'I will not let anyone in, but don't go overboard in the silence. The bride has to wake up in the morning,' she replied, sniggering.

Stolen glances into the marital suite were another awaited custom – naive boys always got caught and were

teased the next morning. The smarter ones would cover the corners of the door with paper and speak in whispers as they peeped. Mumtaz was alert, he had airtight arrangements for his night with the two women. The bride's chamber was next to Mama Jani's room. The *paish bandi*'s narrow room with a door opening into the main corridor came before it. If the bride wished, she could call her at a moment's notice. But it wasn't close enough for the maid to hear the couple.

Mumtaz hurried into the walkway, entered Gulchaman's cubicle and bolted the door.

It was wide enough for a small bed, where she sat with a smile, her lips luscious slices of mangoes. Nawab had spent five long days pining for her mouth.

'Shall I take my clothes off?' she asked. Surprised by her audacity, he stopped in his tracks.

'Why?' was all he could bring himself to say.

'You don't know why a woman would take her clothes off, Nawab Sahab?'

He locked the door to the bride's room and took Gulchaman in his arms. After making love and kissing her till her lips were sore, he stood up, took out twenty rupees from his wallet and placed them in her quivering hand.

She was spread out on the bed, limp and naked, but the money brought her to life. She jumped to her feet and began to count, 'One, two, three, four, five...'

The Nawab had moved away. She went to him and said, 'Have you given all these twenty rupees to me?'

He turned and smiled. 'Yes.'

'Just for this one time?'

He nodded gently.

She clutched his hand and said, 'Then do it once more, just once more.'

Mumtaz was wide-eyed. She, assuming it was his eagerness, begged some more.

'I have given opium to my child. He will not wake up. Please come to me one more time. Twenty rupees is a huge amount. It is enough for a year's supply for me. My husband will be so happy.'

'Your husband?' Nawab was shaken by the thought of another man.

'Nawab Sahab, he is a *darban* at Dulhan Bi's haveli and he gets a meagre stipend. My son doesn't have milk or rice. These twenty rupees would be enough for a year's supply.'

In deep disbelief, the Nawab dropped to the floor. A lump grew in his throat, his tongue and body hardening like a corpse. A long pause later, he asked, 'Do you know where you are tonight and were you aware of your job?'

'Aware? I was sent by my husband to satisfy you well. He told me that you will not give less than five rupees. You don't know Nawab Sahab, it is an honour to become a *paish bandi*. But few are as large-hearted as you.'

'Are you literate?'

'Literate! All I know is that when there is a full moon its beams do not fall on poor homes. This money is more than the moon.' She plucked out a note and waved it at him.

Before Nawab Mumtaz could recover from her story, she began to weep.

'*Paish bandi* is the worst that can happen to a woman. I am such a shy girl. I don't let my husband approach me without dimming the lights. But I was shameless for money.'

Then she threw the money on the ground. 'One has to be so brazen for it. You would have gone to your bride if I had not taken my clothes off, and I would remain penniless.'

Mumtaz unhooked his pearl necklace and laid it at her feet. 'Please return to your husband. This will be enough for your entire life. It's a priceless piece.'

She picked it up and placed it around Nawab's neck. 'The necklace can meet my needs in life but do you know how many poor girls in Hyderabad have to become *paish bandian* to provide food for their families? You are a powerful man. Please promise me that you will erase this tradition. A woman of a suitable age should come to look after the bride, not a girl like me who wants to be with her husband but is sent to someone else's groom.'

'I am alone...Hyderabad is so huge. Gulchaman, how can I remove this tradition from the state?' He fought his desperate remorse.

She was still confident. 'You know a dim ray of light brightens a long tunnel. You are that light, Sahab.'

Nawab Mumtaz heard a girl ask him to walk out of darkness and step into the light. He removed his turban, unfastened it and covered her bare body with it.

3

Tauba Tauba

The Identity Trap

Adolescence had crept up on him. He watched as Simi, snug in a tie-and-dye shirt, wrestled with her cousins. She looked back as Riaz entered, recoiled and covered herself with a blue dupatta.

Riaz had caught a glimpse of her thighs – fresh as oleander petals, silken as cream. Her legs were slim shadows in a gossamer blue *shalwar*. Simi stood still in her azure attire, with Riaz staring, as one in defeat. The spell gave way. He began to move back.

'Rajjo Bhai, you are shameless. You didn't budge. *Tauba*!' she teased.

'I am a man not a child. Don't call me Rajjo. I am...' he almost exploded, then choked on his words. 'If you say

tauba tauba to me again... I am telling you...' He stormed out of the room.

'This *tauba* is eating into me like termite,' he mumbled to himself.

Rajjo had lived his life as a hostage to a moniker and two ordinary words. The past had stayed with him like a toxic companion. He was trapped in the years of his insignificance; the time when he was six, wore shorts or stayed bare, and on occasion, dangled a shirt from his neck. Manju Baji, weary of the other children, would take him to the bathing quarters with her and he would carry colourful marbles with him. She bathed and he played with blues, yellows and greens, his dear droplets of rainbows.

One day, Rajjo lost his beloved marbles in a fight with Anu. So he was Manju's sullen, empty-handed escort, who sat facing a blank wall as she took a bath. The chalky wall being too vapid for the imagination, an exasperated Rajjo turned around. Manju stood under the shower, cold water running along her curves and lingering over her bosom, like his gaze.

Long hair, slick with water and ruffled at the same time, spread over her back and shoulders. He, in his rapt wonder, felt a new, pleasurable swelling. Manju Baji looked towards him as she reached out for her towel. Rajjo stared at her wet, glossy form.

'*Tauba tauba*,' she said, wrapping the towel around herself.

The two words fell like ice on his aroused body and he sank to the floor. She picked him up so firmly, his neck could have come undone. 'Rajjo, it is indecent to watch someone take a bath. *Tauba tauba.*'

Many seasons went by. He never wandered again to the bathing rooms in the courtyard and his family was struck by his strange hesitation. Each time there were marriage celebrations in the home and the men's areas became too cramped, relatives asked him to use the women's facilities, where his mind rang with '*tauba tauba*'.

Riaz had shone as an economics student. His professor had even visited his home to convince his family to send him to England. He was often asked to tutor the girls, but the words '*tauba tauba*' ricocheted in his head. They stuck to him like a sullied memory; they came alive each time he was in the company of young girls, or when he greeted a female guest. Luckily, his retreat from fawning girls was perceived as a knowing pride in his virile appeal, and his sisters were certain that when he deigned to select a wife Simi would be the one. The time came when he began to earn well and the house started resonating with chatter about his marriage.

Rajjo, Riaz Mohammed, was, as Simi said, 'so handsome'. She conjured scenes in her mind – meeting him alone, their conversations and his transition from Rajjo Bhai to Riaz. But for Rajjo, the silence of his room was his universe.

Finally, Simi's long reveries were realized when she

was changing her clothes and Rajjo burst into her room to collect a Thomas Hardy novel, which she had taken from his bookshelf. He had stumbled in unaware that this naive quest would prompt the dreaded '*tauba tauba*'. She was embarrassed. 'What will he think? I was naked and my doors were open!' Then, a thought lit her mind like a firefly. 'Would he want a smooth, svelte bride like me?'

By now, his mother had begun to paint a pitiful portrait of Riaz before the family. She had a handsome, educated, eligible son whose blood ran cold at the sight of a woman. Destined to be misunderstood, in this instance too, Rajjo was taken for all that he was not.

But he found comfort in the aftermath; the marriage chatter went mute and a carefree life in and out of office, bespoke attire, Brylcreemed hair, and other plush, perfect touches airbrushed his world. On one such morning, a few metres away from his home, he had to turn back to pick up his glasses. He entered the house from the ladies' quarters, where Sanober slid from side to side, mopping the floor. Trying to rush past her, he dropped his pen. As he bent down to retrieve it, his skin felt alive again, a new musk wafted through, his own scent too grew more potent.

Sanober's body seemed to let off steam. Sweat slid to her neck, a moist collarbone shone through her ripped neckline. Her midriff wore a sheen brighter than sunlight on glass, soft like freshly kneaded dough. Her smell whirled through him

like a tornado. Now at the other end of the room, oblivious to Rajjo's state, she continued to sweep. So many years into his life, this was the closest he had come to a woman's body. However, in this moment, the persistent torment of '*tauba tauba*' was silent. He collected himself and all the embers within, then shuffled to his room.

'Usman, park my motorcycle,' he instructed on his way up, deciding to stay home for the day. He then thought it best to make an unexpected confession to his mother, in the same, plain way he often spoke to her about buying a new suit. Rajjo was finally ready for marriage, which simply meant he wanted a woman, and not a particular woman.

'Amma, my office colleagues tease me. I want you to find a bride for me.'

The overjoyed mother had no time to waste and presented Simi as her foremost choice.

As he entered the bridal room, a wave of perfumes hit him – roses, *ittar* and *lubhan*. Simi, covered in regalia, sat on a bed of rose petals. 'I am glad she cannot be seen,' was Rajjo's first thought. He knew it was an unnatural one.

Like a ravenous dog, he charged towards her with wanton pangs, turning the lights off. His grip could halt the blood in her veins. In the morning, however, Simi was listless with a

question stuck on her tongue, a tug in her heart. Quiet and aloof, this was not the man from the night. Now that the inevitable had happened between them and it was indelible, he felt empty. Haunted by a formless absence.

'How did you agree to marry me? Was it that day when you saw me undress?' she said with a laugh. But her candour was far from pleasing to Rajjo. If he really were so desperate for her flesh, her thighs would have been bleeding from last night's passion.

A few days later came the news of Simi's pregnancy. She stood on the threshold of motherhood, surrounded by a din of mirth. But it felt alien to her husband, almost like an all-pervasive loss. Rajjo's reticence was immune to her seduction, her beauty, her *singhar*, her newly crafted wardrobe and blouses that clung to each bend of her silhouette.

'Go to a fashion parade, you will be a winner,' teased her friends.

Simi, known for her immaculate grooming, makeup and style, felt discarded and undesirable. In time, Rajjo began to take her on outings, his cold distance standing firmly between them.

'He isn't the same man anymore. The child has changed him,' were bland, banal and gnawing consolations around her.

As her pregnancy matured, her doctor forbade her from taking the stairs and frequent intimacy. Rajjo willingly

obeyed his instructions as young Simi yearned for his touch. Her friends' stories of shredded clothes, bruised bodies, of surrender to desire, burnt through her.

'My garment was in tatters,' someone would say. Simi had never felt so torn and stitched, as if she had stepped out of a tailor shop.

Her mother dashed out of the hospital room to Rajjo. 'You are a father. It's a son!' she announced.

'I am a father. I have a new role and life, yet they still call me Rajjo,' he brooded.

Scenes of his mother calling him Rajjo in front of his son raced into his mind. He was determined not to saddle his son with a nickname. His own childhood memories would pass by with the years.

Simi was sallow with intense fatigue, a faint outline around the moon. To Rajjo, she was lovelier than ever, with a new poise in her demeanour, conduct and speech. Every time she turned away to feed their infant, he would wait for her slight tilt backward to speak to him. Their child grew and so did Simi's chores. She sewed clothes for him, did the washing, tended to his meals and gathered clothes from the washing line in the courtyard.

'Why have you taken so much on, Simi?' asked Rajjo.

'I like to serve my child.'

'But you don't look after yourself. Do you remember how you preened like a model, soaked in perfume?'

Her throat went dry. Even after noticing and saying all this, he had refused to bathe her with his love. 'I came with the fate of nursing an ache,' she replied in a calm but bitter tone. Rajjo wasn't hurt. He knew she felt betrayed. He had failed her, unable to love her the way she deserved.

One evening, he returned from work to find her irate. Their little boy was doused in mud from a pile of sludge in the courtyard, bits of it caked in his hair and toys scattered all over the house. Simi sat cursing her fate. 'How carefree my life was before this marriage! As soon as my veil was lifted, I was shackled with this child. I can wash him, clean him and the house, but this wretched child is always filthy. Had I known this was going to be my fate, I would have waved a fond farewell to this marriage from afar.'

She swept, wept and cursed. 'I had never touched a broom. This rascal will be happy to see me dead.'

'So just one child got to you? You spoilt him. Do you remember all that pampering?' Rajjo made a feeble attempt to lighten her mood.

He moved closer, took the broom. 'Simi, there are many servants here, but they're useless if you insist on doing all the work.'

'Move away! Now you will hold a broom too?' she stung and snatched it from him. He fell backwards.

The once luminous Simi was wrapped in an old, faded sari. In the heat and the haze of dust, a sliver of damp skin showed from her torn blouse, her face and neck shimmered with sweat. Overcome with desire, Rajjo wanted to dissolve in that patch of skin, her smell, her torn blouse. She sprang up to distance herself from him.

'I wore this to clean and then change before you returned. But you are early today. I am so ashamed. What must you think of me!'

He pressed her against him, dizzy with her odour. He bit her cheek, her plump lips and ripe bosom. He tore off each garment and tossed it on the floor.

'*Tauba tauba!* Please stop. We are in the open, and the child...*tauba tauba*, Rajjo!'

Riaz had no time for words. He groaned with each move as he ripped through her once again.

'I am your man, your husband. I will never be Rajjo to you again. I can do as I please, Simi, my love. I still have the power to unveil you, to love you.'

Riaz trampled all over Rajjo and '*tauba tauba*', leaving nothing unsaid as he locked her mouth with his.

4

Zakat

The Alms of Death

It was *chaand raat*. The grand household was alive with customary fervour to see the Eid moon. Each family member began to scramble up to the sprawling roof of the manor. Nawab Zain Yar Jung slouched on a couch and thought of an ancient Arabic verse that echoed his views.

The foolish of this world!
Why crowd roofs!
Be wise with your eyes
As you search for the hidden.
Glance at your terrace, it holds the moon.

Nawab Zain, known for his reckless generosity, had

never bent down in his life. He also held the unyielding belief that Eid was for those who observed all the rituals of Ramzan. So yesterday, as everyone darted upstairs in the hope of an early moon, the Nawab stayed affixed to his recliner.

But this night was different.

'To see the moon of such a holy month heals the eyesight with God's blessings,' the haveli's maulvi said to him.

Eager for a cure, he went to his roof for the sake of his eye ailment. In his early forties, far from the travails of twilight years, Nawab's body had aged beyond its days. However, many ladies narrated torrid tales from his heydays – ceaseless sexual exploits, damsels and orgies. His herbalist had prescribed a valuable elixir of everlasting vigour to him – younger girls for longer years of youth.

This evening, he turned to the sky for relief. Failing to spot the outline of a crescent, the Nawab joined the festivities. His eyes wandered in the direction of the terrace of a tiny house close to the palace. His eyesight was sturdy enough to catch a full moon there.

'How could I have been clueless about such a bequest in my neighbourhood,' he thought.

His faithful Divan stood beside him with clasped hands.

'You never told me that our neighbour was such a vision,' said Nawab Jung.

'Oh Sahab! I never noticed. You need not worry, just tell me and I'll get the girl for you,' he replied.

They returned to his room. Nawab opened a drawer, flung wads of cash at his minion. 'We don't take anything for free. If the girl or her parents are reluctant, give this money to them. It will last for as long as they live.'

In the morning, the Divan put a wallet on the table, stepped back and stood with his hands clasped.

'Sahab, the...the...' he sputtered.

'What? Be clear.'

'Sahab, they are a religious family. They said they don't sell girls but give daughters away according to our religious principles. Then Sahab, they hurled a heavy box at my face.'

The Nawab hissed through clenched teeth, 'So you should've asked them to give their daughter to me in nikah.'

Not yet hardened by the Nawab's fits, the Divan turned into a puddle of sweat. Consumed with fury, Jung called him a *haramzaada*, which, to the master's mind, was the most wounding of slurs.

'They said, Sahab...'

'What did they say?'

'They said, you are old and their daughter is an adolescent.'

'Adolescent!' Jung's head spun with longing. He could smell his own desire. 'But do you think I look old?'

'No Sahab,' replied the Divan. 'You aren't that old. You can get so many.'

The Nawab, deep in fantasy, his tone low, said, 'Yes, that's

true but how can I acquire this girl? She is the one I want, I need.'

'Sir, believe in me, issue an order and I will look after the rest for you.'

'Figure out how many people live in her house.'

'I know, sir. Her mother, a bedridden father, a grand-mother, three or four younger siblings. Ujala is the eldest.'

'Ujala. Light. She is her name,' the lustful Nawab said with a snigger.

'Yes, she can brighten the dark, Sahab.'

'You should not praise her so much. Tell them that Nawab Sahab plans to expand his grounds so they must move out by this evening.'

Divan let his clasped hands hang loose and relaxed his shoulders. 'Yes, it seems like a foolproof plan. After all, where will they go with the family? They'll have to give in.'

On Eid day, Ujala's family came wailing to his doorstep. 'Sahab, we've spent ages at your feet. Where will we go? My old mother cannot walk, and this old man of mine is so ill. I have small children, you tell me, Sahab, where are we to go?' bawled Sakina Bibi, Ujala's mother.

'Our servants' quarters are huge, you can move in there,' he suggested softly.

She looked at her frail husband and the children. Her courage left her.

'Thank you! You are known for your kindness and generosity.'

She was not wrong. There was no match for Nawab Zain Yar Jung's princely benevolence in Hyderabad. He despised taking anything from his friends, relatives and even his family. His role was that of a giver, so much so that even if a precious object fell from his hands, he would never pick it off the floor. Instead, he would ordain that his servants take it and keep it as a gift from him.

A family of wealthy traders that ruled Hyderabad Deccan was a living testimony to Zain Jung's altruism. Their rise in stature and riches began in the Nawab's childhood, when a bag of gold coins slipped his grip and changed their fate. He'd never learnt to bow down, so he asked a servant to collect it. The servant tried to hand it back to him but was admonished. 'We never pick up things that have fallen. Leave this haveli and take the bag with you.'

The rags-to-riches story of this servant and his clan saw them turn into formidable merchants. On the wings of their success, the royal's generosity grew more legendary with each passing day.

Although the haveli's servants' quarters were not ordinary shacks, they were similar to outhouses furnished with all the comfort that was beyond a poor man's reach. Sakina Bibi knew this was a costly barter. The thought of this settlement became a relentless spectre for her. She consoled herself with the Nawab's reputation of being a true giver who would never ask for anything in return, considering his lifelong habit of refusing to accept offerings from anyone.

As days went by, Sakina Bibi grew content. She believed in the Nawab's compassion and was willing to lay down her life for him, the saviour of her family. Her relief was short-lived. It shattered when the Nawab sent for her and said, 'Why do you send your younger children to massage my legs? Send the eldest of your brood.'

Her spirit broke. She recalled the time when he had sent a servant to buy Ujala. Her refusal had set the course of her daughter's destiny. Nawab read the tremor on her face. 'I know what you are thinking but imagine, if I wanted, I could have abducted your daughter. There is no one who could have stopped me.'

'Sahab, why don't you get married? A young daughter's honour is as fragile as a feather. The slightest oversight destroys a girl's future and her family's too,' she pleaded.

'Marriage? Marriage means a lifetime of responsibility. What if heirs are born? Inheritance becomes an issue. No, are you mad?' he thundered.

Sakina began meekly, 'But Sahab, the servant you sent to our house said...'

He stopped her midway. 'Yes, I sent him but that was not the intention. We had a temporary arrangement in mind.'

'Temporary? What is that?'

'Two weeks ago, we were in Jagirpur. How does one survive without a woman for so long? I married a girl there and then divorced her before I left the state. It was a

temporary marriage. Don't worry. If I divorce Ujala, I'll give her enough money for two generations to live in leisure. It simply depends on when I want to divorce her. Also bear in mind that if a woman conceives with me, I ask the hakim to abort the child. He has a medicine for it. I can't allow impurity in the family bloodline.'

'This is forbidden, this is forbidden!' Her screams congealed in stunned silence.

The Nawab continued with his rules and reasons. 'I have only married once officially and my wife is Badi Pasha. All I have learnt is to give and only give. It's why these poor girls who live here can have a temporary arrangement with me and I give them money in return. If I don't help them, then who will? How will they survive?'

A fateful night of the moon had swallowed her daughter and her family's self-worth. Sakina withdrew. Her precious Ujala was sent to him. She came close and the Nawab's was a captive heart. Her eyes and lips were spirits breathing new life into him. A tall girl moulded with milk, as if molten silver was poured all over her, a body that curved like the bends of a river.

Arabic literature had sensuous imagery for women of beauty – 'a cloth draped on a naked body should cover her bosom and hips, every other pore must throb for the cloth.'

'It was written for me and my Ujala,' Zain Jung thought and smiled to himself.

To his surprise, Nawab Sahab did not have to call the herbalist for his staple aphrodisiacs. Ujala transformed his bed and body into a playground. Surging and swelling, he revelled in each moment of fire. Ujala never spoke to him and he didn't miss the conversation.

However, as night after night died into day, some tiny crevice of his heart began to ache for a confession of passion from her.

'You are happy with me, Ujala?' he asked.

She smiled in return.

'Do you need anything? I would give everything to you.'

She shook her head.

'Why don't you talk, Ujala? I am sure your voice is as syrupy as you are beautiful. Talk to me.'

Her response, another coat of the same faint smile.

Gatherings at the haveli were resplendent, with dances, songs and a ceremonial meal of rare culinary grandeur. Nawab Jung's chandeliers and candelabras crafted a cinematic dance of light and shadows on filigreed floors. This night was steeped in sensory pleasures – candlelight, golds and velvets, lavish dishes and a steady stream of wine. And his generosity was in full bloom.

Whenever any of his friends expressed a desire for his mistresses, he was always quick to pronounce a divorce and send her with him. Sometimes, burdened with his favours, his friends arrived with invaluable mementoes, only to

return with them. After all, on no occasion did Zain Yar Jung take a stitch from anyone in his life.

Ujala was brought in dressed in crimson. A curtain of quiet ecstasy fell upon the room and, moments later, rapturous gasps brought it back to life. Drunk and proud of his possession, the Nawab looked on with conceit.

'Such beauty,' exclaimed one.

'Oh! Her poetic grace!' said another.

'A *hoor*. Nawab Sahab, you don't have to fear hell. The joys of heaven are with you!'

'But Sahab, how much did you pay for such a jewel?'

Nawab turned to them with an announcement when, for the first time, Ujala's voice – a voice he had never heard – halted his own.

'You know Nawab Zain Yar Jung's generosity well. He is compassionate, charitable, a compulsive giver who takes nothing. This girl from a poor family is more generous. I can tell you that someone who has never accepted anything in his life took charity from me! I gave the zakat of my beauty and body to this great Nawab. He, Nawab Zain Yar Jung, was the first in my long line of beggars. Today, I ask him, the man who turned down every present, how he accepted charity from a poor girl. I cannot be bought with his riches. He got alms from me.'

This was the voice he had longed for. Just at that moment, his crystal wine glass slipped from his hand and the Nawab

fell on the ground with it. In the blink of an eye, he was lifeless. Ujala watched his fall. She had broken her silence, slaughtered the pride he fed on and discarded the mask of her smile with words that killed him.

5

Zameen

The Floor

He was a tall and grandiose young nobleman with a hollow heart. His horse was his great love and a woman's resistance his aphrodisiac of choice. At present, this rambling manor was busy with his wedding banquet. All duties set aside for fun, Anna Bi's kitchen in disarray, dhols and *shehnai* loud enough to revive the dead, and casting convention aside men and women singing and twirling together.

'Oh my God! How can I manage this chaos! No one cares about the preparations!' She was exasperated.

The baraat was to leave for the bride's home before sunset and time was not on the old lady's side. *Shabdaigh*, the elaborate Kashmiri dish for the bride's breakfast, was far

from the stove and the flour for sheermals was missing. Not even one of the thirty-one bags of dry fruit was ready to go with the procession. Meanwhile, Badi Pasha had begun to arrange an army of servants to carry these delights.

'Before I forget, Chhote Nawab's horse must be fed. Rajab Khan! Where have you been? Take food to the groom's horse,' hollered Anna Bi.

She looked up and saw Chhote Nawab. He smiled and turned to Rajab Khan.

'Feed Rustom, I want to take a round before the baraat to check his stride.'

'Sarkar, he is a faithful animal. He will carry out his duty perfectly.'

'I have told you he is not an animal. He is more devoted than any of you.'

Rajab Khan lowered his head. 'Yes,' he replied and left with the silver *chilla*.

Rustom was snowflake white, lithe and muscular, as magnificent as his master. Chhote Nawab stroked his back, preparing to mount for a quick round.

'Chhote Pasha, please return soon. Your horse has to be decorated,' prompted the tense Anna Bi.

'I will Anna Bi, but don't tell Ammi about my ride.'

'Okay, I won't tell her, but really, who goes out on the day of his wedding?'

It was a pleasant day in early April. But to everyone's surprise, dark clouds brought a heavy downpour. 'I want

more rain, more and more rain,' said the young groom, looking up towards the sky.

In no mood to turn his back on the rain and return to the haveli, he went past Bagh-e-Aam and Shah Gunj Chowk. From here, the vast colony of the Khanzadas came into full view. Many generations of Khanzadas had served his ancestors and now him. When a crop of servants grew old, their children inherited their duties. They were responsible for the daily errands of the imperial home. Rajab Khan was also a Khanzada, in-charge of their stables.

As he wandered through their settlement, he paused at a house with an open area, a canvas awning and a ladies' drawing room. Chhote Pasha dismounted and pinned his horse under the canopy.

'Is anybody home?' he asked out loud.

'Wait,' said a girl. 'Give me a minute. All the clothes on the clothesline are wet.'

Then a girl emerged, soaked to the skin. 'Why were you shouting?' She could tell that the handsome stranger was not an ordinary man. The ongoing rituals of sandalwood and turmeric made Chhote Nawab more radiant, giving him a golden hue. The rings in his fingers spoke of his wealth.

'You, you...' She was trying to speak but no words came to her.

'Yes, I,' he smiled and looked her in the eye. But she was still fascinated by his rings.

'I am the Raja of our state. Now a beggar at your doorstep.'

'Why? You can't be a beggar. We are beggars. We are the ones who crawl on the ground,' she rambled.

He tried to calm her down and said, 'We will see who stands where, be it the sky or the floor, but dear girl, will you let me in?'

'Sorry. Come in, come in, Pasha, it's your house,' she said, making way for him.

When Chhote Nawab passed her, his body tingled. He tried to distract himself with the interior of the house. It was a simple Hyderabadi home, one of the many given to servants, but their squalid condition was a stain on their pomp.

'You live alone here?' he asked.

'No, Baba lives with me. Today he went to work early because the son of Bade Pasha is getting married.'

'You are Rajab Khan's daughter?' He asked in surprise.

She enthusiastically told him all about her father's duties. 'The horse must be decorated. It will take a while. You know, the jewellery of the horse is of silver. This will be an unprecedented wedding. Baba has promised to take me with him. He will come back to collect me after *Maghrib*.'

She turned and picked up an old dress spread out on the bed. 'I have chosen what I want to wear tonight.' Her innocent smile lit up the room.

Chhote Pasha was silent but his eyes said it all. She panicked and faced away from him.

'You got wet in the rain, Pasha. Do you want me to bring tea for you?'

'No, it's hot today,' he said, closing the door and then locking it.

'Why have you closed the door if it's warm?'

Her naïveté kept her from calling out for help.

She, a sculpted body, drenched in rainwater, a beauty with a small nose, long black hair, tufts on her cheeks and pink lips. As the heat in him rose, the rain too became fierce.

Chhote Pasha smelt denial. He grabbed her so tightly that she choked. He kissed almost every part of her – neck, cheeks, eyes, nose and lips. Then his hand touched her face. She pushed him away with squeals of 'No, Pasha, stop!'

As he locked his lips with Nikko's, he tasted the salt of her tears. Chhote Nawab was afire; her protests, pleas and attempts to cry out for help were futile. He was well accustomed to conflict and despised surrender.

'*Nakko*, Pasha, I will die, please don't destroy me.'

He ripped off her kurta, unveiling her carved nude frame. He held her with all his might and laid her on the floor.

She was inconsolable, her arms and legs stunned, like a wounded animal's. Chhote Pasha had never known such a long fight. His conquests eventually gave in to pleasure. But to hope for sweet stillness with Nikko was mere delusion. She hiccupped and prayed to God to save her or take her life.

Chhote Pasha wasn't furious; he was sad for her. 'Why are you asking for death at such a young age?'

'What shall I ask for then? Who would accept me? Isn't it best that I die?' She was ferocious.

He watched her; a figurine of honey and flour. He was desperate to overcome her; for her defeat.

'What's your father's name?'

'Rajab Khan.'

'Where does he work?'

'At Bade Pasha's.'

'What is Bade Pasha's name?'

'I don't know.'

'And Chhote Pasha's?'

'I don't know.' He could breathe with relief.

She wailed and covered her body with her torn clothes like an abandoned old woman on her deathbed. 'Before Baba comes, I will jump in the well and kill myself. My blood will be on your hands.'

He knew she meant it. 'Let me marry you, okay?'

She looked at him, brought her alluring body, tousled hair and a devastating face closer to his.

'Are you telling me the truth?' Her tone smacked of doubt.

'Do you think I am lying?'

'You are such a wealthy man, and we are so poor!'

'What difference does it make? Are the poor not human?'

'Really! You have committed the gravest sin; I am sure God will help you out if you marry me. It's the only way you can be forgiven.'

He pulled her close and said, 'Why didn't you ask me to

marry you earlier? I had to put you through so much trouble for no reason. It's a good thing that I thought of it myself.' He hugged her to convince her of his honesty.

'When will you send your parents to Baba?'

He looked at his watch and said, 'When I go back. It is six p.m. now so they will be here soon.'

'Are you sure?' She wrapped her hands around her body, brimming with the excitement of becoming his bride.

The time of his nikah was set at 7 p.m., after the sunset prayers. A riotous baraat approached the bride's house. As they got to the gate, an avalanche of guests gushed out to see the groom. Ladies peered from the corners of muslin curtains and whispered, 'Oh! What an attractive groom! Like a star fell from the sky.'

Guests then proceeded to the marquee and settled in. A special arrangement for the groom, the maulvi, witnesses, the bride's uncles and other close relatives had been made in the main hall.

After a recitation of scriptures, Maulvi Sahab asked the groom, 'Do you accept the lady as your bride for a *haq meher* of a hundred thousand rupees?'

'*Qubool hai, qubool hai, qubool hai,*' said an unfazed Chhote Nawab.

Meri Kahaani

My Story

Note from the Translator

Wajida Tabassum writes about her life from the time she lost her parents as a little child. This was written when she was twenty-four. She was still new to writing, with just four years of experience. She mentions some of her most piercing tragedies. Two of those are in this collection; the others lost to the tides of time

It has been four years since I set out on the path of words and chose short stories as my medium. Each one presented to you until now does not hold the full essence of the drudgery of this time. When I say this, I do not mean that the stories were toilsome. The path was slow, dark and hard. These stories were my saviours. They carried me out of a murky hole to a meadow. Every heartbeat of mine is theirs, along with all my burdens and sorrows. The truth is that my soul would have slowly and painfully splintered without them.

My hushed sadness and the storm of my emotions is scattered in them. I knew that in the enduring nature of my stories lay my own fragile life and even wishful immortality. The intent of saying this is far from seeing myself as immortal. My work cannot warrant my journey to eternity. Fortunately, arrogance and delusion were not my manacles. Any reason to regard my oeuvre as a collection of grand compositions will make mine a droll story.

I dream. The mind travels to a distant future, towards a time when the stories will be read and remembered as works

of literature. In this fierce chase, I have also felt a double-edged sword hanging over my heart. If it fell, my work would die. These years were hostage to this fear and mine was a wary walk on a barbed footpath. I could not perish.

As I unwrap my life, you will see me as a coward. This tag, with a long history of its own, is inconsequential to me. I often think about your verdict on my saga. But with feet firm on the shore, the intensity of an impending storm remains a mystery.

In all these years, many have leapt at me for scraps of my life. My doors were closed to them. I choose to tell you about myself in a time of blame and societal scorn. As I put pen to paper to sketch my life so far, I want to laugh.

The cruel austerity of my circumstances has compelled me to write this. My pulse is composed with tears and a few smiles. Through them, every piece of me will be laid bare for judgement. This haunts me and I throb with dread. As a ruthless, impartial critic, the thought of framing a dire life with dishonesty is vile. My stories will crack a lie wide open.

This is a Muslim Syed girl from a family where liberties for women were thought odious. My father forbade us to attend school and purdah was our bounden duty. My parents passed away when I was three years old and a paternal uncle persuaded our grandmother to educate us. She relented, keeping a lidless eye on each of us.

My third sister was bright and obstinate, with a great

love for books. She listened intently to every story, which slowly became an obsession. At only three, she forced Nani to enroll her in a school. As time went by, she read, and with it her passion came to a gradual swell.

Several magazines – *Shamaa*, *Jamalistaan*, *Ariyavarat*, *Kaamyaab* and more – could be found in our house. I leafed through them, clutching on to every word. The groceries came wrapped in pages torn out of magazines and I read every line on them. They were more exciting than journals. I took them into obscure corners to scan through the incomplete stories. It felt like all the knowledge in the world was mine.

I have a Master of Arts degree and the impulse to know every word ever written soars as desperately as it did when I was a girl in the fifth standard. However, my passion was tied to our situation. To us, money was a lofty reverie, like a gulp of the sun. The desire to go to markets, explore bookshops and buy literature caved before our meagre means.

It is absurd – and some consider it vile – to reveal that our mother came from a royal family. My father was a prominent lawyer in the city. All my life, I have heard that he earned in millions. He earned and lost. His funeral rites were performed with the help of relatives.

It is hard for me to describe my mother. She was wealthy and came with a dowry attributed to aristocrats; mounds of treasured jewels, five villages in her name. Our grandmother

says that had she saved half the gold, it would have changed the fortunes of the eight of us. But Nani could not preserve even a fraction of that wealth. In those tender years, her constant laments went over my head. Today, they are as clear as crystal, like her jewels must have been.

My father was handsome, unrivalled in the family. When he went out, people turned to look at him. My mother was not pretty, but her hair was long and her eyes lovely. Her description was all I had as we did not have her captured in a photograph. People said her eyes were like the eyes of heroines in novels.

Two years after my mother's death, our father breathed his last. We became our grandmother's burden. Deeply in debt, he had spent every ounce of his resources as well as his wife's dowry. After his passing, our extended family slowly deserted us. Nani was left on her own to sustain us. She was once the grand begum of her household, where storerooms were choked with pouches of cash like bags of grain. Now, she steadily sold her jewellery for us. Some income trickled in from the lands. We lived a spiritless life in grey monotony.

For breakfast, we ate lentils and sorghum rotis, and left for school, our bags burdening our shoulders. As we walked along Camp's Road, I often admired a mansion near the church. From the top of its doorway hung lush vines with vivid flower clusters. Rows of flower pots lined either side of the path leading to it. A large blue motorcar was parked

in the front porch. As we walked up, four giggling, playful children ran out from behind the curtains and climbed in. A maid carrying their satchels sat in the front. They whizzed off in a cloud of dust, which settled in our throats, leaving the taste of its smoke in our mouths.

We walked on and my bag became heavier. I thought about my epitaph: '*Yahaan woh dil dafn hai jo zindagi bhar khushi ke liye rota rahaa.* Here lies a heart that wept waiting to experience joy for as long as it lived.'

In our stretched life, it was difficult for my grandmother to buy several textbooks, but she managed. Sometimes one of us would say to her, 'I want an egg,' or 'No, I want *ghee* and sugar.'

'Ghee and sugar? I get them from a mouse and mice don't like children. Go upstairs and close your eyes,' she would reply.

We listened to her and within minutes she arrived with a bowl of ghee and sugar. The taste of ghee was unknown to us and her tricks worked. Over time, we learnt that her rat's ghee was in fact sugar in water.

I could not buy a book. When I asked for one, she refused and said that such books were unsuitable for girls from aristocratic families. Nani had vowed to keep us away from them and then an accident turned her refusal into absolute restraint.

Our *mama* (nanny and chef) disappeared and Nani, unable

to care for so many of us, searched for another. Many came and were turned away for various reasons. On a sultry evening, the old lady cooked methi ki bhaaji in the kitchen. My brothers were on the *takht* with their homework. The girls had their heads buried in their books and I, with my head against the chessboard and a pencil in my mouth, was working at math. A loud knock on the door gave us a start. Someone had sent a new *mama* and Nani launched into her grilling.

'What does your husband do?' asked Nani.

'He died four years ago,' she replied.

I looked up and saw a child in the lady's lap. My eyes on her, I closed my book and went to the veranda. 'If your husband died four years ago, where did this child come from?' I asked.

It shook my grandmother. She cast a stern look at her grandsons watching the scene. 'Let her read more of those novels! I better not see you with any of those magazines from today,' she screamed.

Chastened and dazed, my fault was beyond the sweep of my imagination. She turned to my brothers. One of them always reacted when she was severe to me. He would tell her to let me read as I was gifted and my future as a writer of stories was in the wind. She said to him that with this state of mind, my prospects were worrisome.

In that instant, my brother yielded and I was helpless. The night was spent in shock as my crime was lost on me. Books

were my source of light and warmth. As the incident comes to mind today, I smile. We were brave in our childhood. But that day happiness in all its forms had abandoned me.

A brief absence made my grandmother anxious. 'Where is that devil?' she shouted. The epitaph echoed in my mind.

As vulnerable as a bird with clipped wings, I wept for hours over the slightest rebuke. Sometimes my shadow frightened me but solitude was my solace. The heart has bled away to infinity, however, my sensitivity is precious and unique to me. Once, when I stepped on an ant, thoughts about its offspring, the particle of sugar it carried, the family it had to feed, made me weep for three days. Time has not changed me.

We lived in a large house that had three levels, courtyards and terraces. Reading could have easily been pursued in secret. But since that day with the maid, my grandmother's vigil was too brutal to slip.

One of my brothers started smoking. Fearful of Nani, he crawled into his blanket for his puffs and was caught after he set a new overlay on fire. I tried his trick and hid in my blanket to read. My attempt was stifled the first night under an airless cover and in the darkness of our room. I arranged for a torch, but the light shone through patches of old, frayed cotton. To lose would have been an insult to my passion. The mind threw new ideas at me and soon there was a simpler way to read. Even though the textbooks lay

abandoned until a few days before the exams, it was an act of deft deceit by me to bury my head in them in the guise of hard work.

A book was always with me. My novels snug in school books, I basked in their language and immersive imagery through the exams too. But misfortune travelled with me. Someone told me to run an errand, I put my notebook on the floor and went outside. A sudden current of air whirled it off like a scrap of paper, uncovering my novel. The incident was narrated by my brother to our grandmother who thrashed me to a half fainting fit. My sense of aliveness peeled off. I lost faith in life and got severe typhoid. It left me testy, more sensitive and even more desolate than before.

I was the sickly, tanned, thin and unattractive sibling with glazed eyes and hair too long for a small frame. The others had good health and golden skin. People called me a witch and a black cat, which sank my sense of self. As I told you earlier, books became a refuge and my friends. In school, my performance was seen as exemplary and pleased teachers accepted my many requests for books from the library. These became the happiest days of my life. I would go through a book in two hours and would immediately pick up another one.

We were poor and walked to our school. As the car from the bungalow on the cemented road drove out, God seemed old and unable to cope with this world. These walks bled my

energy dry. I would still arrive early in school to read more. Our aching feet forced us to voice occasional complaints to Nani.

'Walking keeps one healthy,' she said.

Time has not eaten into my idea of this divine plan, which has scarce joy for a life like mine. In 1947, the Partition ripped through us. We moved to Hyderabad Deccan, where our misery swelled like the sea before a storm.

As a child, I saw my grandmother's wrists covered in heavy and valuable gold bangles. She told us that their weight was *60 tola*. We were out of secondary school. My brothers joined college and as income ebbed household expenses mounted. Our grandmother would go into a dark room with a cutter to sever a bangle. She always parted with a loved piece with a cold face. Strangely, each time she did this, the cutter tore into my heart. The bangles were broken over and over and my heart was slit just as often.

Slowly, we ran out of our ornaments; a few thousand rupees from the land took care of the home and our needs. This was lost to the government when land reforms came into effect.

Our journey from Amravati to Hyderabad was as long as thirteen days and carried an experience of thirteen long years for me, then a girl of twelve. In that trudge, years of anguish seeped in and I aged. It wound up in a city of wretched gloom where we did not have a grain to feed on or a pair of decent clothes. My beloved books were not with

me, we could not afford school textbooks and, at times, Nani had nothing left for our school fees. The youngest and sharpest in the ninth standard, I was also its most ill-fated student. Our life in the village was a grand dream lost in the past.

In Hyderabad, the rules of our library were rigid and the shrunken stock of books hit me the hardest. Once a week, a girl could get one book at a time. All the teachers regarded a dark girl with beautiful eyes, long hair and a tuneful voice as their nightingale. She was known as 'Bengali Mynah', Bulbul and Koel to them. While they had pleasant opinions of me, they did not have a title like hers for me.

One morning, I was humming in class and a girl at the opposite desk said, 'Wajida, please sing a little louder.'

My eyes were fixed on Munshi Premchand's *Godaan* in her hand.

'On one condition,' I replied.

'What?'

'I will sing for you if you lend me your book,' I negotiated.

She agreed. I sang '*Nagri meri kab tak yunhi barbaad rahegi*', and Ghalib's ghazal '*Taskeen ko hum na roye jo*'.

Taskeen ko hum na roye jo zauq-e-nazar mile
Huraan-e-khuld mein teri surat magar mile

(I wouldn't weep over lost peace if blessed with pleasure
of sight,
And if, among the houris of Paradise I see your face)

The next moment, her book was in my hands. Soon after, books flowed to me. I sang to get them and girls from other classes began making similar deals with me – books for songs. I was relentless. The world spread out in an immense space, crowded with writers and varied themes. The ones I read in my harsh circumstances brought smiles and pride. However, as I write these lines, I am sad to think that this, like a sip of air, was a trivial scale.

The city was stoked up in tumult by police action. One of my brothers went to Pakistan and another returned to our hometown to continue his education. Once again, strapped and on the bread line, our family unravelled like a string of beads. My sisters and I were taken out of school. The prospect of an unlettered future tore at me. I longed to return to school, read and learn. In our childhood, my sisters played with dolls and jumped on squares in games of hopscotch and I ran a pretend school with the neighbourhood children.

'Beta, you are Syed – dear to our Lord. He tests those close to Him,' our grandmother would comfort us and herself. Caught in trials, my relationship with the divine powers became conflicted and ambiguous. I pray five times a day and feel like I have paid a great debt to Him.

My grandmother went on a pilgrimage. When she returned, she forced me to touch my ears and apologize for my sin of allotting the title of 'unjust' to the One whom she trusted with all her might and heart. I did as she said, although, I held out.

An overdue bus fee kept us waiting on the street and at school we lined up in the hallways if we were late to pay the toll. I completed my bachelor's and masters degrees in arts as a private candidate. During the intermediate exam, textbooks and food were beyond our reach. Economics was the first test and I sat for it on an empty stomach. My answers are still alive to me. After this was the sociology assessment, and my answers were replete with verses and attacks on capitalism. A woman looked at the sheet and surprised to see the verses she smiled and asked, 'Are you a communist?'

'I don't have a decent shred on my body or any food in me. You call it communism? Then I am certainly a communist,' I replied in a rage.

Those were dark days; layers of gloom coated my sky black. The rich bought grains on the black market, pulses and dates were part of the rations handed out to the poor. For my graduation, my brothers suggested that I take economics instead of Urdu to secure my future. But they misled me. When the question paper was distributed, our professor said, 'All those with economics as a major, please stand up.' There was only one student who stood up and that was me. It was my first academic defeat and I was broken. Floundering in a drought of suitable books, I lost again in my second attempt.

One of our brothers arrived from our hometown on a night when we went to bed hungry. My test was the next

day. Unaware of our financial strains, he said, 'I am starving! Please serve me food.'

He waited for an answer, went out and came back with cakes, pastries and snacks. Hearing his footsteps, I raised my head, saw the fare and slipped under the covers. Before going to bed, I changed into my brother's clothes and washed my only attire. The grime of poverty had blinded me.

In the morning, with sore eyes and a pale face, I put on my sari and set off for the exam. This time, my dream to graduate took form; its shape as solid as my disquiet.

Wiped away by tears, my will to survive gave way several times. Once, when I opened a potion, my younger sister Afroz caught me. My eyes felt like blisters, my hair was thinning and a terrible cough hit me. Our grandmother saw a doctor who predicted grim consequences if I were not nursed to recovery under an unwavering family vigilance. He also prescribed chicken soup, fruits and milk for me, with a tonic and tablets after meals. But prepared meals were scarce at home and his advice to consume the medicines either before or after a meal could not be met. The tonic and pills stayed with us for months. A few days ago, Afroz, Aapi and I were cleaning the house and I threw them out.

A weekly magazine, *Aaina,* was printed in Delhi. It published 'My Memories', a column where writers wrote about an unforgettable moment in their lives. I picked an instance from my intermediate exam days. After setting it

down, I slept in a new lightness as if a traveller in the hot sun was in a dark, cool shade. Words cannot limit my relief. It was here that I began my career as a short-story writer.

Besides my own tragedies, many aspects of life have broken my heart. My words honed them into brazen form on paper and then the piece was sent to the editor. A few stories stirred a sensation. The literary world was not at swords' point, our relatives were. You might think that distant kin are not worthy of a mention. You forget that we were raised by a lonely grandmother. The oldest was only ten years old when our parents died. Nani tended to our wails, upbringing, education, health crises and costs.

No life is ever short of traitors. Abandoned by our relatives to weather brutal times alone, we were bereft of the ones who stand by you through thick and thin. Those who could watch our life grow and diminish with us. I do not resent the clan for it. However, when we were not in school or went astray, our terrified grandmother had to face their refrains. There were times when I bowed my head to her.

After a few stories were published, they flew into feral hysteria and said, 'Wajida Begum has left Ismat behind. Can these stories be read by noble girls?'

'Her work will shock married women.'

'You will see. She will sully her father's name.'

'If my daughter ever wrote such a story, I would strangle her.'

The outcry slowly flowed into Nani's ears. At first, it fell flat. But soon after, a front formed against me. Many poisoned my grandmother's ears during her visit to Amravati. She came back wildly angry at me.

This was when my story 'Teen Janaze' was printed. She came to me with the magazine and insisted that I read it to her. 'I want to hear it. Tell me what your stories are about,' she said.

Dear readers, could I have read it to her? My fault was that I cast naked truths in stories and was not obliged to read them out. My refusal made her suspicious. She believed that the blows being rained upon me held some sway, that the stories were lewd.

Every attempt to defend my work was futile. The moment I held a pen and paper in my hand, Nani appeared and said, 'What are you writing? Read it to me.' A commanding woman, she was not one to be cajoled, misled or evaded. When I told her that it was a letter, she was unwilling to trust me. 'Are letters ever that long? I am sure you are writing a story,' she replied. She then began to repress my correspondence with editors.

At long last, I wrote a note and read it to her.

'Respected Editor, You have requested a story, but I don't have one at the moment. When I do, I will write it and send it to you.'

'What have you said! "When I do, I will write and send it?" Why did you write this?' she shouted.

This ruse of delay did not get me far. She resolved to keep a close watch on my activities. An editor replied to tell me that he had received my story. His words: 'I have it and it is wonderful. The day is not far when you will be a star in the literary world.'

'When did you send this story?' Nani asked.

Her scrutiny was so painful that I gave in and decided not to write. One day slid into another without a word on paper or a drop of ink in my pen. An uncle who leaned on palmistry came to visit us. He saw my hand and said, 'Malika, you have an extraordinary hand. You are destined for startling glory.'

I pulled my hand away with a sullen face. 'Don't embarrass me, Mamu. I have lost the chance.'

In the evening, my grandmother went to see a relative and I broke my promise. I put 'Aag mein Phool' in an envelope and gave it to a servant the next morning. Nani caught me and asked about the contents of the envelope.

The servant answered before I could. 'Mulko Bibi has given a letter and she told me to post it quietly.'

He lit a raging fire and my *aag* and *phool* were on the floor.

An aunt came to the house and said, 'So, she is Wajida Tabassum.'

I think my father named me Wajida Begum, but what royalty did my mother see in me to call me Malika? The family used the name my mother gave me. Sometimes

it became Mulkoo, Milki or Mikki. I was Wajida Begum in school. When I started writing, I changed it to Wajida Tabassum. It was simpler, a way to bring light and laughter into my life. Our extended family has known me as Wajida Tabassum.

The ladies spoke about 'Teen Janaze', and the aunt asked, 'Did you write this story?'

Too scared to confess, I lied, 'No, it was Fikr Tunisvi's work.' Fikr Sahab had edited it for *Shahrah* magazine, so his was the first name that came to mind.

'But the story was printed with your name.'

'Well, you see, that's the way it is done...' I stammered, burned deep into a strange space where my story should belong to someone else.

'My dear, I advise you for your own good. You belong to a family...' said the aunt as she made her way out.

I almost flayed her alive. 'If we are vilified, it is us not you. Where were you when my father died and my grandmother was alone? Now we have a name. Why did you decide to accept us?'

This was not me. It was Wajida Tabassum, the storyteller who wanted her legacy. Some incidents are radioactive in nature. People scurried away, afraid to talk to me. Their lies and betrayals were played out behind my back.

Earlier, another relative had been skinned by me. When wedged in a barrage of insults, I flew open. 'This time, it's

just you. Even if my father returned from his grave and asked me to forsake writing, I would disobey him.'

The uproar peaked four years ago. My distant relations who saw me as a shame, claimed Wajida Tabassum as theirs.

'Wajida Tabassum is my niece. She is a brilliant girl.'

'Wajida, my relative, writes sparkling stories.'

'Her father was a dear friend. She has made her family proud.'

All their voices were frozen for me. They brought neither joy nor pride, or even sadness. I wanted to deny any connection with them, my tormentors. This shift in sentiment and my fame had not calmed Nani. She felt that Wajida Tabassum and her stories were strangers because I had not read them to her. Afroz narrated a story and the word 'love' unhinged her. She had her reasons.

'Love with what, with whom? So, she writes love stories,' she said.

The dark corner was still my writing lair. Bano, Jilani Bano, came to meet me and asked where my 'literary work' was woven. She was aghast that I could breathe in a narrow, dim cleft. To show her my tools, I also took out a broken pen, a rusty knife, a small inkwell, a piece of brown pencil, and some fresh ink stains on new magazines.

She wrote to me when she was back home.

'Dear Wajju, my advice to you is that you leave this spot and go under the open sky. If sunshine comes into your stories, they will be magical.'

I replied to her.

'Dear Bano, I don't need the validation of a larger source like the sun. I am the light in that dark place.'

She was not alone. It was a choir of many famed writers. I wanted to steal the sun in and become that fireball. However, my stories are about families. Like the author and their characters, they hover within walls.

The world is awash with other subjects and novelists. Women who recognize social concerns such as peace, war and strikes can put infinite themes on paper. However, a woman trapped in a traditional house such as me, not familiar with shopping centres, cannot assume a solid grasp of conflict, peace, communism and politics. It is simple. Hyderabad Deccan is my world and gangsters in Karachi are beyond the sweep of my wildest aspirations.

Krishan Chander can write with blinding flair as seen in 'Mahalakshmi ka Pul'. A tale of two universes of the privileged and the poor. He knows Bombay. His gender allows him to explore the globe, giving a vision to his work, and no one can say to him, 'Have you ever seen the streets of Bombay or chanted slogans with protesters?'

However, Chander does not know that a biryani recipe is short of red peppers. He cannot prepare biryani; I cannot write 'Mahalakshmi ka Pul'. Like our lives, we exist in two different genres. It is reasonable to access spheres known to us. They do not scare us and our readers will not be deceived.

I am often asked to step out of the confines that surround me and my stories. To travel and explore, to nurture my work and make it immortal. Many say that my tales are too similar to each other and I accept that they are. But would you believe I got on a train for the first time three years ago? It was an experience I will treasure with clarity. This is the expanse of my world. If my brother had not married a girl from Nagpur, travel would still be a flight of fancy.

The moment I stepped on the platform, my grand fantasies shattered against reality and turned to dust. The bridge seemed to shake when our train passed over it and I feared it would dip into the stream below. A Christian lady next to me said that she had never seen a coward like me.

Perhaps, my stories will journey out of their walls when the time is right for me to navigate without fear. After all, life has just begun to stir a little for me.

A few of you have criticized my work and I do not mind if more of you do. When you honour it with praise, you breathe new life into me. My characters affect you in different ways. It eases my pain and softens the adversities of giving birth to them. They are friends who come to me. I wrote the longest tales in one sitting. 'Sheher e Mamnoon' is one of them. The characters are intimate to me, my life and my heart. It was hard to release as my heart ached. Readers told me I could not write another to match it.

'Gulistaan se Qabristaan tak' has been the most tragic story so far. 'Kaalay Baadal' was also traumatic. Its desperation and turmoil chased me. I was awake for many nights, thinking about the losses caused by and for monetary gain. I questioned the sacred, the injustices at the heart of troubled human creation. The doubts about the purpose and origins of our existence overwhelm me. At each thought, I turn pagan. If nature rested on me, the world would be less broken and less intricate. But these circumstances are crushing and bitter. This world is the soul of irony, where survival and laughter reside within us. Our inescapable truth.

Anyway, forgive my digression. I wanted to tell you about the remnants of my work left on me as scars. Many other tragedies – 'Saatwan Shehzada', 'Paandaan', 'Ladki Bazaar' – hurt because they are real.

My first story appeared four years ago, on 6 September 1955. All along, tributes poured in and I broke away from dissuasion. But I sense a bleak future. My name does not mean much and is not well received. However, I believe that failure is the path to perfection. When I look back, the passion to chase hope and carve a space tears through the yokes of the past.

Returning to your complaints about the monotony and want of contrasting themes, my deep desire to see the world closely is the elusive gold at the end of the rainbow. When it

is within my reach, the change will be yours. This bird is new to flight and can only promise clever diversity over time.

In our literature, forewords have become customary. I feel they lean our readers in a certain direction, which is worrying. Why do we need a renowned name to endorse our work to the extent that critique is printed on the dust cover? I have many letters from celebrated writers, who applaud my work. Many of them are dear to me. They would compose a preface in an instant. But I disagree with the idea. The foreword to me is a diversion for the reader's mind and a tool of cheap publicity. When someone wants to move ahead, they should walk without a crutch. Even if that means taking an uneasy road to the last stop.

You must wonder about my perception because I have addressed all your thoughts about the stories. I want to be close to you.

In the end, I will say that I travelled softly with moist eyes as Wajida, to become Tabassum, a smile. The long and weary path to this name is wet with my tears. This is my story so far.

Wajida Tabassum
29 December 1959
Hyderabad Deccan

Greed

1

Faakhta

The Dove

In her blanketed, conventional world, Maina was a stranger. She rarely read any literature, but her pen wove dreams on paper, and one of her stories found space in a magazine. Her mother hid from appalled visitors, ashamed.

When the uproar of disapproval subsided, Maina learnt English, subscribed to *Asmat*, an 'improper' magazine, read adult novels like *Beheshti Zevar* and *Deeni Masail*, which were unsuitable for single girls. *Daulat par Qurbaaniyaan* was the first book in her home. She smiled in the face of frequent reproach and elders accused her mother of blinking at her daughter's libertine choices.

She wore saris in place of voluminous, modest kurtas, vibrant studs instead of her mother, Mumani Bi's, delicate

earrings, necklaces rather than pendants and visited homes with bare wrists. A worldly woman, Mumani Bi was oblivious to the widening gulf between her daughter and the family. However, Maina had quietly shaped her own future.

'Girls and daughters-in-law are the life of a home. Why is your home so wayward?' they sneered every time Maina diverged from tradition.

That afternoon, Maina took a nap in Shabbir Mian's bed. She left it warm, a dimple in the pillow and her long braid imprinted on wrinkled sheets fragrant with her smell. Later, when Shabbir Mian came to his bed, he caught a familiar scent, as seductive as a breeze filled with the smell of jasmines. He stepped out to call Munni and Rashid.

'Munni, Rashid, come here!'

Munni ran to him, pulling her hair away from her face, and asked, 'You called for us, Abba Mian?'

'Beti, did you sleep in my bed?' he asked softly.

'No, we didn't. We have been playing outside for a while.'

'I have been outside with Munni. We haven't climbed into your bed with our dirty feet. Apa was in your room,' Rashid replied.

Shabbir Mian recalled that Mumani Bi ordered special perfume potions for Maina's bath, and she was always more fragrant than a new bride.

'Khaansaama, lay the table, Mian is here,' said a voice on the staircase.

Shabbir Mian, Mumani Bi's nephew, had become closer to her after his marriage. Mumani Bi never took a step without his advice. And whenever a new dish came out of her kitchen, Naseeban Bua brought it to Shabbir Mian before dinner time.

He had settled his property disputes and moved from his village to a house next to Mumani Bi; she meant more to him than his own mother. His wife, Rafia Begum, and their two children visited Mumani often. Rafia, almost thirty, became a close friend of Maina, who was only sixteen.

When an officer sent a marriage proposal for Maina, Rafia Begum turned it down, much to Mumani Bi's outrage.

'The boy earns well and has all the qualities I want for my daughter's groom. But Rafia's approval was more important to you. Have you turned against me, girl?' scoffed the indignant mother.

'When I am not willing, you cannot force me,' retorted Maina. She knew about the boy's glad eye and Rafia Begum had simply conveyed her own refusal.

Not long after, Rafia went into labour with her third child. A midwife was summoned. In the hands of an amateur, the circumstances swiftly spiralled into an emergency. Shabbir Mian went to call Maina, leaving the ladies mystified. She had saved Channo Khala's son when he fell into the pond by holding him upside down as water spilled out of his mouth. Mahto, the gardener, who was once bitten by a snake, was

another witness to her remarkable alacrity – she had given him neem leaves to chew until the potency of the snake's venom waned. Therefore, Shabbir was hopeful that Maina's ministrations could save his wife.

He stood near the purdah and asked Naseeban Bua to call her.

'Tell Chhoti Bi that my wife is not well...'

Naseeban Bua screamed, 'Mian, are you in your senses? You are asking a virgin...'

Before Naseeban could say more, Maina rushed to the door.

'You must go and bring the lady doctor, here is her address.'

Shabbir Mian turned to run but stopped. 'What will she charge? There is no guarantee that she will come for Rafia! What should I do?' He could barely stand, his legs too weak with anguish.

Maina leapt out of the room. 'Let's go, let's try to persuade the doctor together.'

Rafia survived but lost her child. Once again, Maina was reprimanded and Mumani Bi did not speak to her for several days. Shabbir Mian's visits became more frequent, Maina always offering him a silent *adaab* with a slight wave of her hand. She ignored her mother when she chided her for not using 'bhai' to address Shabbir.

'You have changed after all the education. This is not

a proper *adaab.*' Mumani Bi thawed with time. Maina responded with a smile.

The perils of another pregnancy were conveyed to Rafia Begum by her doctor; having a third child would be a threat to her life. But two-and-a-half years later, she was again in fatal labour. Shabbir Mian lost his wife and the unborn child. Though he'd been aware of Rafia's coquettish flirtations, fond memories of their shared life flashed through his mind. He looked around his quiet home, at Munni and Rashid, and sniffled.

Mumani Bi was inconsolable at the *chehlum;* she mourned for Shabbir Mian and his children's future. In spite of the nubile girl in her home who had the city's gaze on her, she came to the forlorn father's rescue with an unconventional offer.

'Mian, there is no one to look after Munni and Rashid. Stay with us in our home.'

Shabbir Mian politely declined. A simple man, burdened with responsibility and emptiness, he became as quiet and impassive as a wax statue. When Maina got the chance, she would go to his place and wash the children's hands, comb their hair and feed them breakfast.

One day, Shabbir Mian visited Mumani Bi with his children.

'Mian, they say the death of a wife is like a blow to the elbow. It hits hard, but passes just as quickly. How long will

it take you? You are young, there should be someone to look after you and your children,' she said.

'Please don't talk about my agony. What will a stepmother do to my children? I will not be able to bear it.' His voice trembled. 'Look at my house! Every inch is covered in dust. When I return, there is nobody to wash my face or to fetch a glass of water for me. The children suffer with me.'

Maina melted and said, 'Move into our place. Amma is here and the children will be comfortable and happy.'

'I would but...' Shabbir Mian drew back.

Mumani Bi watched the scene as Maina continued, 'You are afraid of the elders, aren't you? You should only consider your own situation. Dogs will bark. Let them.'

This went on for a few days. Mumani Bi's clan observed merciless purdah; it was against their custom to even look at a photograph of a man. But she prevailed and Shabbir Mian moved in.

Maina spent her days with the children and slowly their grief died down. On occasion, they would see Maina in finery and say, 'Ammi would dress like you.' Or, 'These earrings are like Ammi's.'

Shabbir Mian lived there like an outsider. Deserted by laughter, he spoke softly. Mumani Bi's fears faded and she was certain that her Maina would not catch his lowered eyes.

'As a child, my daughter chirped like a mynah so I gave her the most suitable name,' she said to Shabbir as they chatted in the courtyard.

'Really? It's a lovely name and she laughs so gracefully.' His tender praise made Maina's heart flutter violently. She was not a shadow to him; his words were reassuring and warm, like home.

After a few days of an intense, unexplained fever, Mumani Bi took her last breath. The usually marble-eyed Maina spent her nights weeping in dark, secluded corners of the house. She often thought about all the proposals acceptable to her mother but cast off by her and the ones she liked that were discarded by Mumani Bi. She had to take her desire to see Maina in her new home to the grave with her. As her Bade Nana said, 'A howling dog is a bad omen, and if it was within earshot, a *sadqa* should be distributed.' The tragedy of Mumani Bi's loss struck their home days after dogs in the neighbourhood howled through the night and Naseeban Bua's milk turned sour on the stove. She said a prayer for forgiveness. Now, after the loss of the shield that was her mother, unsparing family elders turned Shabbir and Maina into the talk of the town.

The chatter eventually subsided, Shabbir Mian stayed on in Maina's house. They were attuned to a life under the same roof; he did not make overtures and Maina was reticent. After work, he would rush into his room. In the summer he took his newspaper and sat on a stool in the courtyard, and in winter a sweet voice announced his arrival with, 'Khansaama, lay the table, Mian is here.'

One afternoon, Arshad ran in, rubbing his eyes.

'Ammi applied kohl to my eyes when they itched,' he told Maina.

'Oh! Why didn't you tell me? I will do it for my little angel.'

She prepared the kohl and began to slowly roll a silver stick in it when he stopped her. 'Ammi said that a metal should not touch the eyes.'

'Alright, I'll use my fingers.'

Some of it stained her fingers so she casually lined her eyes with it. In the evening, she welcomed Shabbir Mian with the usual, 'Khansaama, lay the table, Mian is here.'

An exuberant Arshad dragged Maina to the table. 'Look, Abba Mian, Apa applied kohl to my eyes! Can you see it?'

'Yes. Your apa cares so much for you.' He answered as he ate dinner.

Shabbir Mian made his way to the courtyard to sit on the stool and Maina approached him with the newspaper. 'I took it to read, without your permission.'

Shabbir Mian looked up to reply, but made a surprising remark. 'Your eyes are so beautiful.'

He took the newspaper from her and turned to it, his face as blank as a poker player's.

Maina, swept away with disbelief, hurriedly turned towards her room. She tripped over her sari and fell, Shabbir Mian bolted to catch her, his arms around her body as warm and soft as a dove.

'You don't walk carefully. What if you break a bone?' he said, lifting her up. Her head near his nose made him shiver.

That night he read a blank newspaper.

Maina came down with a flu and Shabbir Mian missed her voice when he returned in the evenings. Three days went by. Shabbir Mian wanted to check her condition but stayed away, thinking colds and coughs were too trivial to fuss over. Then he remembered the instance when he was ill and Maina had advised him to get married so that someone could care for him.

However, overburdened with the favours of Mumani Bi, and later Maina, he dispelled his thoughts and convinced himself to find a boy worthy of her.

'God forgive me! I did not enquire about her health. She loves my children and looks after me. I live in her house! How can I be so unmoved!' he gasped, flung away his paper and darted off to see Maina.

She was better, caught in a struggle to remove her sweater as the pallu of her sari was entangled in it. So, with her back turned to the door, she placed her *aanchal* between her knees and whipped the pullover off. In her doorway, Shabbir Mian broke into a sweat. Maina smelt his unease. Catching her breath, she turned around and saw him walk away.

For the next few days, she lay in bed in shame and left the room after a week. Her way with Shabbir was that of a new bride. She shied away from his gaze only to look at him from

the corner of her eye. He was silent, but her familiar scent reminded him of the time when her smell was all over his bed. It now informed him about her affection and attraction towards him.

Whenever Munni and Arshad insisted, she would lie in his bed to read to them until they fell asleep. Months passed and their routine remained the same. Maina smiled, the children played in the evenings, and then, 'Khansaama, lay the table. Mian is here,' brought everyone to the dinner table.

'Maina, these clothes smell stale and will be infested with carpet beetles soon. Put them in the sun,' Shabbir Mian said one morning.

She brought out all the suitcases. Shabbir Mian was at home that day and the children joined her. Maina opened the largest suitcase. Each of Rafia's belongings, from jewellery to glitter, was still in its place. She took out every piece with care and placed it on the floor. Munni and Rashid made no mention of their mother.

'Do you miss your mother?' she asked.

'No, you take care of us and love us so much,' they replied in unison.

'But I cannot take her place.'

'We think of you as our mother,' Arshad replied.

Maina blushed, tears rolled down her face. 'Really?' she whispered.

'Of course.'

She returned to the suitcases, and deep inside one she found a glittering *kalipoth ka lacha*, the symbol of union. She picked it up and looked at the clock; it was a quarter to ten. This was Shabbir Mian's usual time to go out. She bounded to the door, paused by the stairs for a moment and looked at the *lacha* in her palm.

'Please listen.'

Maina, with a corner of her pallu near her mouth, downcast eyes outlined with long lashes, and a svelte body neatly framed in a plain sari, stunned Shabbir Mian. The girl before him was the one whose scent he nurtured; the one he kept safe in his dreams. As his eyes swept over her, he saw the *kaalipoth ka lacha*, the beaded necklace that women wear signifying their married status, in her hand.

'There is everything in the vanity box except for *massi*,' she giggled and ran out of his sight.

In the evening, as he entered the house with a packet of *massi*, she, in a tone that signified their coupling, said, 'Khansaama! Lay the table. He is here.'

2

Joothan

Leftovers

In Nawab Sarkar's imposing residence, the circle of life spun against nature. His desire was insatiable and his heart as cold as an executioner's. He wanted his servant, Kalwa, to be well fed.

'You bastard! Are you massaging my feet or playing with them! Where is your energy? We feed you, but your lethargy flows through your blood!' He kicked Kalwa with all his might. He fell to the ground, far from the royal bed.

Kalwa gathered some strength and returned to his master. He had stiffened with fright, his limbs numb, as if he had lost his pulse. A hearty meal was a distant memory.

The rambling haveli was home to several tiers of attendants. Milk mothers, or *annas*, were a cut above.

Although poor, they came from respectable families and were treated grand because they served the begums and the wellbeing of aristocratic infants lay at the heart of their existence. *Mamas*, as guardians of the kitchens, prepared delicacies for the Pasha. Their appetites were first quenched with the tasting and then with sumptuous leftovers. Servants, maids, gatekeepers, gardeners, betel nut vendors and janitors hovered on the bottom rung. They brought their own food or received meals under Bade Sarkar's supervision, measured in spoons with the depth of a dent in a knife.

Servers in the men's portion of the house were discards. With a monthly salary of two rupees, their food came from their pockets, which meant they only ate at home. Sometimes Kalwa went home late, hungry as a wolf, to lentils and coagulated rice. Then again, Kalwa was luckier than the others. His proximity to Bade Sarkar made him the secret keeper of the stately bed and he brought many virgins to it. Bade Sarkar learnt about his mastery of persuasion from a complaint he once made about Mushtri, a young maid who was the *paandaan* keeper. He had sent Kalwa to get a *paan* for him. Kalwa returned and asked Pasha to send Hameed in his place.

'Why? Do you have henna on your hands?' the Nawab rebuked.

Kalwa, scratched his head and replied, 'No, but Mushtri...'

'What does Mushtri do?'

'Pasha, she is not a good woman. She takes my hand and places it on her breasts. Maulvi Sahab said that a man's touch is reserved for his wife.'

Bade Sarkar was so lost in lustful thoughts about Mushtri that the rest of Kalwa's plea did not reach his ears.

He gave Kalwa a rupee, which was half his allowance, and ordered him to persuade Mushtri to come to his room for the night.

Mushtri's arrival propelled Kalwa to the status of the landowner's confidante. From Khana Baagh to Moazzam Jahi Market, from Chaar Minar, Kotla Aali Jah, Meer Alam Mandi, Punchi Buraaq to Mehboob Ki Mehndi, every night Kalwa presented Bade Sarkar with a pubescent wonder from a different area.

Time and trade honed Kalwa's manoeuvres; he no longer settled for a mere rupee. His eulogies for each catch got him two to five rupees and sometimes, as much as ten rupees. He was able to send money to his poor parents in the village, who were struggling to reclaim their land. But he still ate at home, where his wife waited with lentils and thickened rice. However, gradually, when Sarkar ate from the elaborate tray of food that was brought to his room, he, satiated with wine and woman, took a few morsels and told the servant, 'Take the tray back and give it to Kalwa outside. This is his share in the *joothan*.'

The servant took the tray to Kalwa with spite. 'Take his *joothan* with you and return the tray.' This was Kalwa's only source of a nutritious meal, but whenever Bade Sarkar attended a dinner or got a fever, he sent word to the ladies not to prepare his tray, and Kalwa went home to homemade dal and rice. He conveyed his sense of deprivation to Sarkar with a weak massage which often earned him a powerful strike from his master. However, of late, his reactions were no longer about the massage, it was the dwindling supply of moonbeams.

His master was now addicted to having a new girl in his bed every night and as time went by Kalwa began to run short. He wished for a marketplace of girls, like Mir Alam's Mandi in Hyderabad, famous for its fresh and abundant vegetables. But girls could not be bought, they had to be lured with money.

As Begum Sarkar became invisible and forgotten, Kalwa swept every crevice to illuminate his Nawab's bedroom with the joy of a woman. The hapless servant reflected on the weary ways of his world where everything was dispensable – food, old clothes, shoes were given away without any sentiment, as were precious watches after years of keeping track of time, but a storm broke out when a maid took the place of a wife.

The Nawab wanted to barter that space night after night. Tonight, the emptiness aroused the fury of a crocodile in

him. 'Are you scared because of money?' he asked Kalwa, who was yawning from fatigue.

Kalwa saw this as his moment to end the game.

'Yes, Pasha, you are right. I didn't ask you because you would suspect me of stealing money. Her mother asked for twenty-five rupees.'

'Twenty-five rupees? Is she from a mythical place? From *koh e kaaf*?' Bade Sarkar roared.

'Yes, Pasha, she is. If you find her unworthy, change my name from Kaleemuddin to Kalwa.' Then, he walked over and asked, 'You know, the magic of a vessel formed from red sand is that it turns a splash into the sweetest tune. She is like that melodious vessel.'

The Nawab stood up, took twenty-five rupees from his wallet and threw them at Kalwa. 'Go and get the girl now!'

Kalwa grabbed the money with both hands and ran home to his wife.

'Sukoo, Sukoo, where are you?' he shouted as he approached the door.

A restless Sakina rushed over to him from the courtyard, 'Why are you screaming?'

'How delicious would you like your food to be? Chicken, biryani, qorma, chutney, naan?'

'Ch... chick...?' stammered Sakina in awe. 'You have lost your mind with hunger. What can I do! We don't have money for *dal-chawal* tonight. It is a *faaqa*.' She wept.

'It's not a *faaqa*. It is a banquet. Look at this.' Kalwa tossed the notes into the air. Sakina pounced on them.

'Just do me a favour and you can have the money. This is a year's salary.'

'What kind of favour?'

Kalwa led her to their room and selected a white muslin kurta from the alcove. He took off the soiled one on her.

'What are you doing? Can't I change myself? Have some shame!' she yelled.

'Sukoo, you are *maal*. Come with me for twenty-five rupees.'

Then he put the white kurta and a dupatta on her and brought her to Bada Sarkar.

When poverty forces a poor girl into diaphanous muslin, it turns Nawabs into scroungers. At first glance, Sarkar hankered for the heat of her youth, the sparkle in her fine eyes, the warmth of skin; that night, he was a beggar. The light from his chandelier spilt on the silver button strip on her chest; he saw goblets of *kheer* on either side, aching to be touched and tasted by him.

He turned to Kalwa, whimpering like a hungry dog. 'You asked for very little. I would shower that amount on her.'

When Sakina scrambled out of his room, her face crimson with tears, Kalwa was waiting in the bushes. As he saw her, he jumped and dragged her out of the house. They got into a rickshaw and he asked to be taken to a large hotel at Nampally Station, which was open late.

He took a seat, ordered chicken, biryani, dessert, yogurt, chutney and naan. With the luxurious dishes before him, he looked up at his wife for the first time that night.

'There is a long night and a long life to cry. First, eat enough food to live. It's your earning.'

A pang of sorrow shot threw Sakina, spears flew from her eyes as she looked straight into his. She took a spoon and started to beat him with it.

'What are you doing? You know we may never have chicken again. You will forget the taste of biryani too. See, you have everything you can imagine. Eat it. You have not eaten all day.'

She took a deep breath, put down the spoon and stared at the food, then plunged in, bringing one fistful after another to her mouth.

'You have slept with me for so long. Where is the harm in a night with Bade Sarkar? It brought us a year's wages.'

Hardened by hunger for the most merciless of blows, Kalwa had traded his wife's honour for an abundant amount and for his scrupulously crafted plan. He would whisk Sakina off to his village, live with his family and spend his days with dignity as a farmer. Sarkar's insults and abuse were behind him.

They spent the next two days preparing to leave, with Kalwa absent from the haveli. But the Nawab was breathless for Sakina. He arrived at Kalwa's doorway in his massive carriage on the pretext of asking about his health.

Nawab Iqtidar Yar Jung's arrival at a servant's house was a monumental event and the neighbours came out to see him and his pageantry. Kalwa had gone to the market and Sakina was at home.

'Sakina, come and see, a huge carriage of a Nawab is outside your house,' a neighbour called out.

Sakina ran out and her eyes met with Nawab Sahab's glare. His heart was beating in his throat; he continued his act.

'Which is Kalwa's house?'

'This is his house,' answered one of his men.

'Then who is this girl in his house?'

'She is his wife, Sarkar.'

Nawab Sahab looked at Sakina and then at the people of the area.

'That bastard committed a fraud with me for twenty-five rupees! Let him come back and I will take his skin off!'

He turned to Sakina, 'This guard will stay at your home and when your husband returns, send him to me.'

Kalwa shivered like a naked man covered in sleet as the Nawab attacked his fragile body with a cane.

'Why did you do this to me, you bastard? When you had such a beautiful wife, you could have sent her for free. We have fed you for years, it was your duty to provide beauty to me,' growled Sarkar.

Kalwa was silent.

'Now, return my twenty-five rupees and I will sleep with your wife every night for a month.' Kalwa did not say a word.

'This is not enough. You must endure more. When we are in my room, you will sit by the door so you can hear me with your wife.'

Then Sarkar sent for the servant who served dinner to him and said, 'From today, don't give my *joothan* to him. He has deceived me and he should know what it's like to be hungry.'

Struck by the terror of hunger, Kalwa felt fierce and fearless. 'Yes, from now I will not have his *joothan*. Sarkar will have mine. Every night.'

Bade Sarkar's staff fell from his hand and landed at his feet.

3

Kaalay Badal

The Shadow of a Grave

Shakoor's was a face creased with tragedy. He was simple and devoted to Hameeda, a feisty woman maddened by her love for her husband. A life free of hunger was his obsession; he also slept in a grave.

One night, a soft clangour in the room woke him up. He looked up and saw Hameeda rummaging through a shelf.

'Why are you awake? It's so late,' he said, narrowing his weary eyes.

'My stomach hurts. I can't sit or sleep so I am searching for *ajwain*.'

Shakoor jumped out of bed. Short of breath, he asked, 'Pain in the stomach?'

Hameeda turned and said, 'Yes, but why are you so loud? It's just a stomach ache.'

'Which month is it?'

'If I include this one, then I have just completed eight months.'

'So, you are in your ninth month now?'

'Yes. And you can think too?' she teased.

'You are a silly girl! Even though it's the beginning of the ninth month, it is a full term. I say the baby will be out in a few hours. Your pallor says so,' declared Shakoor, like a seasoned midwife.

Hameeda screamed in his face. 'Really? I am pale? We eat every second day, so should I be pink?'

Shakoor ignored her mockery. 'It's so sad, I will lie in the grave on the day you give birth. What a contrast! How can I be in a grave when my heart is with my child?'

The burn of his words was intense. Hameeda gripped her stomach. 'For the last time, stop this sickening work. You have done it for too long. Now, as a father, think of your child, if not me.'

'My queen, I wish I was a landlord, but I am not. We need the money.'

'I don't care. The truth is, from now on, I will not let you step into a grave. Look at what this work has done to you. It is killing you. See your pale face, the dark shadows around your sunken eyes. Your cheeks have melted, your chest is

weak, your skin is a thin film over a web of veins. I don't want such a life.' She was seething.

'Then go and starve,' he said angrily.

'Yes, I will starve. This life is an inferno.'

Shakoor, singed by her rant, said, 'You are giving birth to the child of this ostrich, what will you feed it? My head or your own?'

Hameeda stroked her belly, 'Baby ostrich! How can you call it that? I will feed it whatever I like. What if I do not feed it? It will not make much difference.'

'Will you starve it to death?' he asked.

She smiled. 'Why would I do that? This pregnancy brought me all the happiness in the world.'

'Is that why your face is as yellow as a mustard field?'

He was still talking to her, when Hameeda felt dizzy. Shakoor leapt up to hold her. He put her on the bed and asked, 'How do you feel, Meeda?'

'I don't know how I feel, but I want you to promise me... For my sake and for our baby's, you will not go to the grave from tonight.'

'Meeda, I have told you many times that if I stay at home we will not survive. When all the doors closed on us, I chose this. Do you think I don't love you and the child?' He held her hand.

Hameeda wiped the sweat from her face, she yelped with pain, and said slowly, 'You have not recovered from your

last night in the grave. How do you spend twelve long hours there?'

Shakoor touched her stomach.'It's for our provisions.'

Her face turned sallow. Anguish surged in her gut; she always thought of his work as ominous and it made her tearful. Then Shakoor softened. 'Had you asked me nine months ago, I would have given it up. Now we will be parents, how can we let the child starve!'

'Then...' Hameeda gasped. 'I will sell the baby to the doctor. We will have five hundred rupees and you can start your own work with the money. God will give us more children.' She sobbed, as if she had looked death in the face.

'What did you say? Meeda, I have longed for a child and you threaten to sell it? How can you be so brutal?' The thought made Shakoor come apart.

'You cough all night...' She was in the middle of her sentence when she let out a squeal. Chachi ran in from the courtyard and Shakoor took to his heels to find the midwife.

While on his way his mind couldn't help but wander to the condition of his life. 'I went to the city and worked in a factory for four years, and like with many other workers, they asked me to leave. The village did not have a job for me either. Defeated by the vagaries of life, I sleep in the grave. The darkest of clouds have loomed over us, fell ferociously and passed. These dark days of sacrifice will heal. Imagine selling my infant! Does she really want to destroy me?'

The sight of the midwife's house broke his stride and his desolate contemplation.

The midwife cleaned up and left their room; Hameeda and Shakoor looked at each other with their bundled up newborn next to her. He had breathed life into Shakoor.

'We have been blessed after seven years, Meeda! I don't know how to thank God.' He was delirious with joy.

Hameeda, still embroiled in the same argument, was caustic. 'Love your son, don't you? What if he asks for something?'

'What can he ask for? He can hardly gurgle,' he said with a laugh.

'Babies can't speak, but their bodies can. Your son says that he wants his father to live. Leave this work. God will give you another chance.'

'Why fight on the happiest of days? I will leave it when you get me a bag of money.'

'And if I arrange for the money today?' She asked with strange assurance.

'Yes! How many times should I say it!'

At that moment, they heard a familiar voice outside. 'Today, at 11 a.m., Shakoor Naik will sleep in the grave for twelve hours. A living man buried in a grave! Come, see it to believe it. Just for four paisas!'

With each announcement, the memory of his first steps towards the grave came back to Hameeda. They were the hardest to bear; it was as if the mud still clung to her fingers. Shakoor chortled, 'The wife of a brave man is scared. I have done this for three years, Meeda.'

'You do this twice a month for twenty-two rupees! Who gave you this idea?'

'My stomach did.' Then he picked up his shawl and went to shower.

An hour before his time to leave for the vault and its soil, Shakoor asked Hameeda if she had fed the baby.

'No, Chachi said the milk will only flow when you are full,' she murmured.

'Then, I'll get dry fruits for you in the evening.'

He leaned in to kiss Hameeda and his child and walked out. Her heart sank deeper with each footstep. She glanced at the baby; rosy cheeks, a dark head of hair, dry lips, he rested on his forehead. Slowly he became a blur and eventually she could only see a bag of money in his place. She reminded herself that she had a treasure, and that five hundred rupees would help Shakoor open a garment shop.

Every month, a doctor visited their village in search of illegitimate children and orphans. In their neighbourhood, Taajay Uncle had sold his child of five months to him and had six more children. Her immediate concern was to save her man. Shakoor was now a faint sketch of his once sturdy form.

Once a tree bears fruit, age is its final season. Are you worried that your Muslim child will be in a Christian family? Wherever he goes, he will always be your child. For grave sleepers, money is religion. Hameeda put her hands on her ears to quieten her mind, and then on her heart.

She got up and stumbled. The baby was only a few hours old, still wet, eyes closed, not suckled at the breast. Hameeda wrapped him in her sari, peeked out of the door to see if Chachi, now in the kitchen, had her back to their room. She took a quick breath as she left the house and walked onto the street.

The Christian doctor was in the red-stone house next to where Bade Zamindar lived. She saw the red door and darted towards it. The doctor was on the front porch, knitting. She smiled at Hameeda and put her needles and wool away. Hameeda placed her baby on the table in silence and spread her arms.

'The price of my motherhood?' she asked, her face streaked with tears. The doctor lowered her glasses. 'Illegitimate child?'

Her question made Hameeda's face change colour. She was pallid and sweaty. 'Whether a child is legitimate or not, a mother's love does not waver.'

The doctor walked over to the chair. She gently uncovered the child's face. 'Oh, it's a boy! How much for him?' she said with a smile and sat down.

'Not a penny under five hundred rupees,' replied Hameeda with an air of frosty resolve.

'Sometimes, we get babies for free,' said the doctor.

'This is my first child, born after seven long years of marriage. He is the light of our home. But I have chosen to extinguish this beautiful incandescence and come to you to sell him.'

She bent down and said to the doctor, 'Madam, I am doing it for my husband, who sleeps in the grave for money. It is a performance, but if it continues he will die. So, by selling the baby, I will earn for him.'

The doctor listened patiently, went inside and returned with a stack of crisp rupee notes. Hameeda took the money, looked at her son, and turned away. 'How long will you stay here, Madam?'

'I will leave in the evening. The longer your baby stays here, the more you will yearn for him,' she explained to comfort the fraught mother.

'You can feed him.'

'No, I will not feed him. I cannot afford to change my decision.' For a moment, Hameeda's heart felt faint, and a dark mist fell over her eyes. She pulled herself together, took the money, walked away and then ran back to her sleeping son. 'Madam, how will you feed him? How will you raise him?'

'I have raised many children. Your child will be fine.' She was gentle.

'Can I come to the station with you?' Hameeda asked, her tone singed with desperation. She felt the blood in her veins dry up. Unsteady and broken, she sat down with her head on her knees.

'I don't mind if you come, but do think about yourself,' said the doctor.

In the evening, a horse-driven carriage came to the door, and they went to the railway station.

'Madam, please treat him like your child and not mine.' Hameeda pleaded. At this painful moment of final parting between a woman, a poor mother and desperate wife and her life, Hameeda's body became hard and cold like that of a stale corpse.

Soon, the train chugged farther and farther away. Hameeda's chest hurt from breasts heavy with milk, tides of piercing emotions gushed through her. She was alone, her arms without a child, again, and her baby lost to an unknown destination. She stood by the tracks for hours, then remembered the money wrapped around her waist.

But the thought of Shakoor's pained reaction to her suggestion of selling their baby and now of his sorrow and anger tore her apart and Hameeda's agony turned to fear. After all, she was guilty of the inconceivable, of selling their first born, the child he yearned for. Her lingering consolation returned; if she could save her husband with the money, in time their home would come alive with their large brood.

Whenever Shakoor slept in the grave, the village people marvelled at the feat and rejoiced in a small fair. She thought about going to the ground and taking Shakoor home. A soundless house would break him, but a bag of money could bring distraction and, more importantly, hope. Hameeda told herself that she had shut the door firmly on their dark fate. She had traded her child for light, and in a year or two she would have another baby.

The burial ground was a scene of tumult. People ran from one end to the other, their cries echoing in the air. She watched on in a daze.

Someone nearby screamed, 'Go and tell his aunt and his wife that this poor man suffocated in the grave! How can we send the body to his home?'

'What happened?' another asked.

'I don't know. Remember Shakoor Naik? The man who slept in the grave? He had a cough in the morning. He performed here to scratch a living. I heard he became a father today!'

She dropped to her knees in shock, her clothes now dirty with the soil Shakoor had lost his life to, and he seeped into her.

4

Shaadi

A Promise

Everyone is a hero in their story, but Yousuf Mian was not one in his. He was pious, never had a drop of alcohol in him, lived his life between college and the haveli, and played cards with friends behind closed doors. But, a perfume haunted him.

On entering the ladies' area for the first time, Yousuf Mian saw Sandal. She sat bathing a baby with Paris soap, drenched to the flesh, her dupatta on her shoulder and *shalwar* rolled up to her knees. She leaned forward; her cleavage was half bare. Yousuf scurried into a corner. However, the scent and Sandal hung in his mind like a noose.

'Bibi, please take a bath. I have arranged everything for you in the bathroom.' Sandal begged Jahan Bano, who, sunk into her bed, was absorbed in a novel.

'Bibi, please! The water is warm.'

Annoyed by Sandal's incessant pleas, Jahan Bano threw the novel aside and dragged Sandal onto the bed.

'For God's sake, Sandal, don't make me suffer this torture every day.'

'Is taking a bath torture for you, Bibi?' Sandal was exasperated.

'No, Sandal, I am not in the mood today. Why don't you smear the ubtan on yourself and bathe in my place?' Jahan Bano giggled.

'And after that?' Sandal teased.

'Set your wedding bed.' The two burst out laughing.

'No, no, forgive me. All of these arrangements are for you,' said Sandal shyly.

Jahan Bano was a few months into her marriage. Whenever she came to visit her parents, her mother laid out elaborate preparations to make her daughter feel like a new bride. Spices were soaked overnight in water and *shikakaai* was boiled for Bano's hair, the finest sandalwood paste was prepared for her body.

Sandal, Jahan Bano's childhood friend, was tasked with lathering her with these. She loved Jahan Bano and the duties thrilled her. Bano had wanted to take Sandal to her

marital home, but her mother felt it was like presenting the son-in-law with a second wife. In this home, Sandal looked after her; she was more of a friend than a maid and servants envied her rank.

'Sandal, have you taken Jano to bathe yet?' Badi Begum's approaching voice made Sandal slam the door.

'Listen, Bibi, run to the bathroom and close the door, or Badi Begum Saheba will be livid with me.'

'Oh God! Why is it so important to take a shower every day! Go and tell her I have a cold.'

'Think about it, why would I soak spices and mix perfume with *ubtan* if I knew about your cold. Don't get me into trouble.'

'You talk such nonsense, Sandal. If my mother scares you so much, why don't you take a bath in my place? I will tell her that I took it.'

She hauled Sandal by the hand, shoved her into the bathroom and went back to her book. She read briefly, then joined her brother and husband for a game of *gilli danda* in the garden.

The *ubtan* made of turmeric and saffron made Sandal as radiant as a glowworm. Her wet hair spread all over her back, she searched for her clothes then changed her mind – they were sullied with sweat. Jahan Bano had not thought of bringing fresh clothes for Sandal when she had pushed her inside. She wrapped a dupatta around herself and began to sneak into the room.

As she came out of the dressing room, the pale pink dupatta glued to her wet body, Yousuf Pasha stood in front of her. The sight of him made her shudder. However, she knew he was a gentle person, the older brother of Noor and Jahan Bano, who treated Sandal like a third sister. But it did not make him less of a man. His eyes were out on stalks when he saw Sandal wrapped in the gauzy sheath.

'I came here to hide from Dao Dena, who just beat me in the game...' He swallowed his own words. Sandal tried to cover herself with her hands.

Her perfumes cast a spell of furious passion on Yousuf Pasha; he saw satin calves, plump lips, golden skin, a statuesque frame. The scene silenced him for a while. Then he lifted her up and laid her on the bed.

'Sandal, I will put pearls in your hair, I will sacrifice everything for you. We will get married,' he whispered, his breath warm and heavy.

Sandal knew that every maid had to submit to a moment like this and it could have been anyone, if not Yousuf Mian. To her, the words, 'I will marry you Sandal,' spelt sweet surrender.

The lace coverlet on the bed was torn to flakes. Yousuf Mian took a small piece and put it in his pocket. He cupped her face and said, 'This is a souvenir of our love. I will carry it in my pocket, close to my heart.' He opened the door and gingerly walked out of the room and her life.

Yousuf was the eldest, but his father wanted his young daughters married before him. While he believed that girls should keep away from schooling and professions, he encouraged his son to graduate before marriage. Nawab Sahab was also averse to marriage engagements.

Badi Begum wanted the grooms of their daughters chosen more wisely, but Nawab Sahab listened to all the suggestions and did as he pleased. The daughters were sent off with the first in line for their hand.

Yousuf Mian, armed with a degree, awaited a bride. Salamat Yar Jung was Nawab Sahab's childhood friend, but there was not one attractive soul in his family. Zulekha, his youngest daughter, was different, with eyes like emeralds, a wide forehead, black hair down to the waist, fair and tall. She was educated and fluent in English and Urdu.

Nawab Salamat fixed a handsome sum of two hundred thousand rupees for each daughter, with valuable presents for his sons-in-law, leaving little reason to delay the weddings. Relatives gathered at the sparkling haveli to witness Yousuf's proposal. And Salamat Jung's acceptance sent streams of clamorous delight through the home. Preparations began instantly, the first being Mumani Jan's arrangement for a wall clock in the *dalaan* so servants could be summoned on time.

Through these days, Yousuf Pasha stayed away from the women's quarter; he had erased all memory of his passion

for Sandal. But she was ready to battle for his promise. She, a maid trained in the art of being a lady of the haveli, had learnt grooming and etiquette well from Abba Huzoor's daughters and had been taught by the same tutors. Her wardrobe consisted of silk ghararas, pyjamas, kurtas – Sada Jahan Bano's and Noor Jahan Bano's second-hand clothes. But her beauty put the heiresses in the shade. Families of repute came knocking on her door to ask for her hand and Sandal refused.

Mumani Jan's son visited on Eid and when he saw Sandal serving sweets in elegant attire, he forced his mother to propose for her. But Mumani declined.

Baba Huzoor would laugh and say, 'Begum Saheba! No one is poor by choice. Why turn down good prospects?' His son, Murad, an accountant, was lovesick and decided that he alone would marry her. She had encouraged his advances until her moments of passion with Yousuf Pasha.

Sandal waited for her young Pasha, keeping their time close to her heart. In all this while, she met him once. After the evening prayer, she heard him call all the maids and servants by their name, asking them for ways to remove the black ink stain from his silk shirt. Murad, with a faint grin, advised him to rub chalk on the stain and left. Everyone who was called by their name departed; she stayed.

'There was just a stain on your shirt that you wanted to get rid of, but do you remember what you did to me? Who

will remove this stain?' The question played on her lips. Suddenly, Yousuf Mian turned around and looked at her blankly. Sandal thought that upon seeing her, he would remember that day, that piece of lace. 'Why are you so skinny?' was all he said. And with that, in the haveli's din of joy, her love story was snuffed out.

Salamat Yar Jung's family was as large and grand as Yousuf Pasha's. The groom would receive five hundred thousand rupees, a private house for the newly-weds, sets of diamonds, rubies, emeralds in gold, a bed of solid gold, and a hundred and twenty-five dresses. The wedding invitations were printed on gilded paper, engraved with the names of the bride and groom. Nawab Salamat sent his list of priceless presents on the day of the mehndi to inform all the guests about his largesse.

Every home in Hyderabad was invited to the opulent wedding. People poured out of cars, buggies, carts and rickshaws. The extravagance of the bride's family spread out on one side, and the groom's procession shone like a carpet of silver, heaped with jewels and surrounded by policemen. It went past Chaar Minar to Moazzam Jahi Road, where the nikah, set at five in the evening, had to be postponed by two hours.

Mumani Jan took out her present of jewellery for the bride. When she opened the box, she realized that she had forgotten the diamond neckpiece at home. She called for Nawab Sahab and told him about the incident.

'I left the most valuable piece at home. Please go and collect it. I can't trust anyone else, so you must go.'

Nawab Sahab got home and entered the bridal suite next to Mumani Jan's room. He hastened to open the cupboard, took the set out and was about to leave when he heard someone weeping.

'Who is crying here?' he whispered under his breath. He went to the bride's room and found Sandal at one end of the decorated bed, crying.

'Sandal! What happened? Why aren't you at the bride's house with everyone else?'

Sandal never spoke directly to Nawab Sahab. Today, she ran to him and held him tightly. 'Baba Huzoor!'

'Why are you crying?'

'Baba, if I was pregnant, I would have told everyone that he is the father of my child and now he is married to someone else. But I am so unlucky.'

'Did Yousuf Pasha say something to you?' asked Nawab Sahab in a low, soft voice.

'Say something?' She almost let out a yell in rage. 'His words ruined my life! He promised to marry me. I trusted him, otherwise I am as solid as a rock. I am not an ordinary woman.'

'Yousuf Pasha promised to marry you? Are you telling me the truth?'

'Yes, Baba Huzoor, I never lie and that's why I haven't said

a word until now. My chance to become a bride is lost, Baba Huzoor.'

Nawab Sahab put his hand over her mouth, 'Don't say that Sandal beti. Didn't Begum Saheba give you a dress for the wedding?'

'She did, but I don't want to wear it.'

'Go and change into that dress.'

Nawab Sahab held the jewellery box in one hand and Sandal's hand in the other as they stepped out of his car. Nawab Aitemadud Daula called for his wife.

'Place all the jewellery and the bridal set on Sandal,' he ordered.

When Begum Saheba tried to protest, he told her to obey him. 'You know what I ask you to do is good for everyone.'

He pulled Yousuf Mian from the ornate sofa, took him to the women's section and removed Sandal's veil.

'Yousuf Mian, do you remember her?'

The son was quiet.

'If you were passing time with her, I would not intervene. But you promised to marry her! This is a man's word,' said Nawab Sahab, pointing to his own lips.

'Once you give your word, you have to keep it. I want to hear it from you. Will you marry Sandal and promise to make her happy? Zulekha is a nawab's daughter. If you do not marry her tonight, she will have many suitors. But will you be happy after you have broken Sandal's heart?'

Yousuf Mian glanced at Sandal and Nawab Sahab caught his look of acceptance. He took his son to the men's area.

'Now, Sandal, the bride, is my daughter and as her father, I will not allow you, Yousuf, to marry her for less than a hundred and twenty-five thousand rupees. Do you understand?'

Envy

1

Adam aur Hawwa

Adam and Eve

The train ate into the distance as it wandered along the rails.

Chhuk, chhuk, chhuk… it ran.

'Well, if I jump out of this moving carriage, what then?' the smiling woman asked.

With his gaze fixed on the newspaper, the man replied with a touch of loathing. 'Uh, we'll see when the time comes.'

A while into the journey, he folded his paper and put it away.

'What if I fell off this train?' he said with a beam.

She looked at him for a moment and, the next instant, she leapt out of the window.

2

Dhanak ke Rang Nahin

The Rainbow Has No Colour

There were a few things on his mind. One of them was his bondage. Rafiq lived in his ancestral home, where the mood was dark like a morgue. If Rafiq Mian could change one thing about his existence, he'd leave this life behind and chase his dreams and his love.

One morning, with the achkan on his shoulders, he was on his way out when Hoori ran towards him. Playfully wrapped in a curtain, she said, 'Mamujaan, there isn't a single piece of betel nut in the *paandaan*.'

'Let it be. Who even eats *paan*?' he replied.

'But Ammi Jaan has asked for some.'

'Bi Banno, these are unnecessary expenses.'

Then, he saw her slippers. 'Pink slippers?'

Hoori flapped her delicate feet to show off velvet mules.

They got him thinking about who they could belong to. His mother was old; his sister was a widow clad in white and he had never seen Zehra Dulhan wear them. He thought his niece had resurrected them from Apa Bi's dowry items.

'Whose slippers are you wearing? What if they get dirty?'

'No, they will not,' she said, hiding her feet behind the curtain.

'I am sure you will tear them.'

'Why are you so concerned when Shakoh Baji isn't?'

'Shakoh Baji? Who is Shakoh Baji?' Rafiq asked with a quiver in his voice.

'The lady inside in a green sari,' Hoori said, and threw the curtain aside. 'Mamujaan, she has beautiful, colourful clothes and boxes of bangles, slippers and sandals.'

'But you shouldn't use someone else's things, Hoori.'

'She is my phupi!'

'Apa Ji's sister-in-law?'

'Yes.'

'But I have never met her.'

'That doesn't mean she can't be my aunt!' the girl replied indignantly.

'So, you want betel nuts for guests in the house.'

That's when Apa Bi came looking for Hoori, who ran away to avoid being caught.

Rafiq Mian returned home after half an hour and went to

his room. This time, he did not lie on the bed or take a deep breath; he hung his achkan and sang low. Hoori dashed in, 'Did you bring the betel nut?'

He caught her by the hand. 'You are chirpy today. What if I whacked you?'

'Give the *chaalia* to me,' she chuckled, holding out her hand for the betel nut.

'I will take it myself,' he said.

Rafiq followed her out of the room and she disappeared behind a curtain. In the veranda, his brother Annu Mian's wife was breastfeeding. He moved away. He heard Hoori teasing her little cousin Aslam in a room near the courtyard.

Rafiq put the packet of betel nut on the *takht* and said, 'I brought the *chaalia* but I can't find the *paandaan*.'

The curtain at the door of the corner room swung, and he saw a rainbow in motion.

'Ammi has *paan*, I apologize for the trouble,' said a syrupy voice.

The green border of her sari got caught in the *paandaan*. She bent to untangle it, turned around and went inside. Her silken, rose-tinted heels caught his eye.

In an opaque, starless sky, Rafiq no longer felt like a rag hung out to dry. Bathed in the hues of early spring, he had sprung to life. Her feet skipped across his mind; he put his hand to his mouth, afraid to open his heart. '*Dhanak ke*

rang... The colours of the rainbow...' he thought. There were no sweeping winds or rumbling clouds, nor the heady scent of blossoming buds invading the air to announce the silent spring that washed over him. But, in that moment, he was in love.

When, from behind white muslin curtains, *paans* came to him, he would ask, 'Hoori, who makes these?'

'Shakoh Baji.'

Rafiq asked over and over again, and a rankled Hoori repeated, 'Shakoh baji, Shakoh baji, Shakoh baji. Have you heard me?'

'Does your Shakoh Baji chew *paan* all day like an old lady?' he teased.

'She has ruby lips. But what do you have to do with her *paans*?'

Rafiq Mian knew his astute niece and so he turned away to avert an uproar. However, this was the first time in his home that he received five *paans* in a day. He had never wanted one before; now his mouth was a shade of rust.

A week later, Rafiq was absorbed in his papers when his mother came to see him.

'Amma, are you worried?' he asked.

She gripped her knee and sat down by the wall to rest. 'Your Apa Bi's sister-in-law and mother-in-law are in the house.'

‘They have been here for nearly a week,’ he said, trying to sound nonchalant. ‘But today you are quiet. Why, Amma?’

‘No. You are just suspicious,’ she replied with a faint smile.

‘You cannot hide anything from me. I will think you don’t love me.’

‘How dare you say that! Who else can I love in this world?’ She was rueful. ‘In the peak of your life, you have aged beyond your years.’ She gently caressed his head, the strands of white a sore sight for her.

‘Amma, if I were born a thousand times, I would sacrifice everything for you and my siblings,’ insisted Rafiq, hurt by her words.

‘Don’t say that, my son. You should be married, with children.’ She sighed.

‘Tell me, why are you here at this hour?’

‘I have run out of ghee. We need it for eggs and parathas for their breakfast.’

‘I will arrange it. Why do you fret?’

‘We have enough mouths to feed, with your brother and his family around. The Ganga does not flow in our house!’

‘Don’t taunt Annu so frequently or he might leave, Amma.’

‘If he wants to go, he can,’ she snarled.

‘But my peace too will go with him. He was the apple of Abba Mian’s eye. He told you on his deathbed that Annu was

another form of him. If you pick on him, how will our father rest easy?'

His mother had watched Annu's contribution and role in her household closely. Rafiq's pleas did little to thwart the tirade about her feckless wastrel of a son.

'He will mature with age,' reasoned Rafiq.

'He is a father of three. What about their expenses?' she said angrily.

'I will send Baqar in the morning to fetch ghee.'

As tears streamed down her face and settled in her wrinkles, her unease rang true to him. The old mother had watched her eldest son enter his twilight years on his own and the other one have a child every year without the means of supporting them. Her only daughter had been widowed in her youth. Apa Bi's husband's family could not support her and her five children so she had come back to her mother's home. Hoori was born seven months later. In this nightmare, Rafiq Mian was her only pillar.

After Abba Mian passed away, Amma had sold her jewellery for his education. He'd pursued a law degree and fulfilled his family duties. His attempts to make Annu a doctor, however, had failed. Much younger than Rafiq, Annu had left school before matriculation and lived on pocket money.

Years slid by and their blanched home had trundled along in humdrum routine until the day Amma Bi decided to rescue Rafiq from this drudgery.

'We have seen several tragedies and now I want Rafiq Mian's wife in the house. Why don't you want a bride?' she had asked.

He'd laughed, 'Have you chosen a girl?'

'Now that you have agreed, consider that I have.' She beamed.

'But I was talking about Anwar's wedding,' Rafiq had replied.

'What? Annu should marry before you?'

'Do you think my situation allows me the luxury of marriage?' he sighed.

'Believe in yourself. The wise stand strong.'

'Yes Amma! I don't trust myself. What if my wife is defiant?'

'A woman is like a shoe. Don't stress about it so much.'

'No! You cannot disrespect a woman. She is a crown, she is sacred,' he protested.

'So, you will not marry?'

'I didn't say that. I will when the time is right. Apa Bi's children look to me for their needs. Then, Annu and his marriage and...'

'When a man is distressed, he needs someone to bring solace to his heart. A mother is a mother, and a wife is a wife. Their roles are different.'

Conflicting thoughts had tormented Rafiq. He wanted a wife and children, but the image of a family collided with his fear of quarrels at home. While Anwar could eke out his existence, Amma, his sister and the children only had this roof. Besides, Hoori was already on the threshold of adolescence.

The tinkles of anklets and bangles were forgotten melodies there. He'd shared his worries with Amma, and his truth had crushed her. She chose a girl from the family for Annu and he married Zehra Dulhan. They'd settled into a room by the courtyard. The bride's adornments clinked as she walked through the house and clattered loudly at night.

The home had turned into a vibrant mustard field with elated faces. On days when Rafiq Mian had a fuller wallet, he'd come with saris, bangles, earrings and bracelets for Chhoti Dulhan. She would sit surrounded by fascinated children who talked to her for hours. Some ten months later, Zehra had spent a night squealing in pain. Annu and Rafiq sat at the door till dawn, Amma paced nervously and fourteen hours on Annu had broken down with fright. A baby's cry ended their ordeal. Heart in mouth, Annu ran into the room.

Rafiq's heart had pounded with joy as his mother whispered, 'You are a *taaya* now.'

On the same day, when he'd looked in the mirror, the white strands near his ear became spectres of his isolation. He wanted a hand, a colourful *aanchal* over his face. Then,

the passive manner of Zehra Dulhan came to mind. It made him think that if he had married, his wife too would've been as calm as a wax figurine. But, once again, Rafiq Mian turned his back on his desires.

The house was illuminated for the birth of little Aslam, and the household had gone up in cheer. When Zehra Dulhan entered for *godh bharai* – a traditional Indian baby shower – frenzied delight for the newborn that swept through the family had even brought their widowed aunt to participate in the rituals.

Zehra Dulhan had asked, 'Apa Bi, must you put this garland on me? Can't Hoori perform this with a simple, light string of flowers?'

Her measured words were not lost on Apa Bi, who, in her love and mirth for her brother's child, had forgotten that she was a widow covered in the shroud of ominous superstition. After all, the customs were performed by wedded women and she could not become the reason for any misfortune to befall her brother. It had torn up Apa Bi. Her nerves were in a knot, the garland fell from her hand and she'd passed out. Zehra had also shaken Amma. Her dear son Rafiq's solitude was already an abscess in the old lady's soul. But, in that instant, she understood and accepted his fears for Apa Bi and the children.

Zehra Dulhan's comment had brought greater anguish. Annu had begun to take offence at Apa Bi's slightest oversight and his anger often caused her to shed many a tear.

Rafiq Mian had approached Amma. 'My wages are limited. We don't have another source of income. So my marriage is a far cry. It means a larger family to support and provide for.' She had wiped her eyes and hugged him.

Annu, spoiled by Rafiq, had shunned obligations. Their hearth was held by its eldest son and his resources. But he could not buy peace. Emboldened by her new eminence as the mother of the family's only heir and the impact of her pointed question to Apa at the *godh bharai*, Zehra was on a warpath. Each day broke with her fury.

Aslam was a lovable novelty for Apa's children. They teased him, played with him and fed him, but when he cried Zehra flew into a rage.

'Where is the fun in making my infant cry?' she would scream.

'We made him cry! He eats so much. Someday, he will shout like you do,' Hoori replied, sharp as a knife.

Chhoti Dulhan spat fire, 'You talk like your father left you a huge fortune. Don't you eat here too?'

Before their brawl spiralled into fresh tumult, Apa would dash in to strike her daughter.

It was during those testing days that Tahira, Zehra Dulhan's younger sister, had visited. An attractive girl, she was easy to talk to. Even though Rafiq Mian was in the *mardana*, he had caught glimpses of her. Amma was weary of the drama in her house, but Apa Bi insisted that Rafiq marry Tahira.

'Zehra has shown her true colours. What if Tahira does the same?' Rafiq had questioned.

'My brother, I will find a sweet girl for you,' she had assured him.

Rafiq had picked up an apple from the basket nearby. 'This looks lovely, but do we know its taste till we eat it?'

Apa had no words.

Dulhan prepared *mirchon ka khatta saalan*, a sour curry spiced with green chillies. It was relished by all. Old Amma Bi, who had been unwell for ten days, ate quietly. Then her moist eyes, sniffles and calls for water spurred Zehra on.

'Ammi Jaan, aren't you happy with it?'

'Bibi, I have blisters on my tongue and diarrhoea,' she replied, and stuck her tongue out to show the sores.

'You knew Amma was ill. Why didn't you make another dish for her?' Annu asked.

'Am I the cook? Have I taken charge of looking after everyone? We should separate our kitchen!' she shot back.

Rafiq and Amma watched in silence, but Apa said her piece, 'Dulhan, you entered the kitchen for the first time. Baqar carries out our chores. Amma and I cook and make rotis.'

'You mean I live a royal life?'

'No. But cooking a curry does not make you our servant.'

Dulhan howled and cursed. Rafiq politely said, 'Apa Bi, if they want, they can have their own kitchen.'

'They don't have a decent income,' goaded Amma.

A tense Annu Mian glared at his wife, and pleaded, 'Bhai, please don't take her seriously.'

Zehra was not one to stop. 'After all, Rafiq Mian is the eldest. Where is Abba Mian's wealth? How can one brother be a lawyer and the other illiterate?'

In the dead air, Rafiq Mian sat, singed. Annu looked at him with remorse. 'Bhai Sahab! Ignore her. She doesn't realize that when kitchens separate, families and hearts part too.'

'Yes, Zehra, we should live under the same roof with large hearts,' Rafiq responded.

After the putrid episode, Rafiq moved into a room in the men's portion of the home. Within the walls of his room, as blank as the canvas of his life, he spent his time buried in paperwork and in his thoughts.

He tried to patch up his fractured world. He closed his eyes to see a gentle face, hear a soulful voice. As his mother said, there came a time in a man's life when only a woman's affection and tender body could bring relief.

Now, glimpses of those pink slippers would be the only glimmers of life he experienced. He began to dream and a wingless heart took flight. Rafiq swayed when she

sauntered by. The moment Shakoh turned and her rosy heels were in view, he surrendered to an indefinable force. His heart sang a new song, an ode to a living statue in his temple of ecstacy.

Rafiq and Shaukat – his *dhanak ke rang* – had not met. When dinner was laid and Amma Bi said, 'Raffoo Mian, Come and eat,' or Hoori shouted, 'We are waiting for you, Mamujaan!' he entered shyly. Shakoh's fragrance told him of her presence.

Ever since the ugly fight, Zehra cooked separately. However, the family shared a *dastarkhwan* to christen Annu's new son. Meat was sent to relatives and hearty dishes were prepared with paper-thin rotis and desserts.

As Rafiq put a morsel in his mouth, he gasped, 'Such divine qorma! Have you cooked it, Amma?'

Amma looked at Shakoh and smiled. Shaukat, looked up and met Rafiq Mian's eyes. He quickly replaced his plate with a bowl of dessert.

'Amma, I don't think you have ever made firni as delectable as this.'

His mother laughed. 'We all know that Shaukat has laboured all day in the kitchen. So why do you praise your mother?'

This time, Shaukat looked at him and didn't turn away. She was fair and petite; a thick braid ran down her back. Rafiq, having wiped his bowl of dessert clean, suddenly got

up and left the room. He fell on the bed and took a deep breath. Then he looked long into his eyes in the mirror.

Rafiq Mian decided to make Hoori his confidant and asked, 'Hoori, does your Shakoh Baji soak her heels in rose water?'

Hoori laughed and went inside. 'Shakoh Baji, Mamujaan thinks you dip your feet in rose water!'

Shaukat looked at her feet with wonder. She touched her heels and blushed. 'Tell me, why am I laughing?' she asked, gently touching Hoori's chin.

'I know. You wear pale slippers to show off your heels so Mamujaan can admire them.'

'What do you mean? *Tauba*!'

She put her arms around Hoori. 'Now you will ask why I blush? Why are my eyes so deep? How do I answer your questions?'

One evening, when the ladies were curled up on the *takht* in the *aangan* which was the courtyard in the house, Amma mentioned Shaukat's marriage.

'Have you fixed Shakoh's wedding?' she asked her mother.

'She is twenty-two years old, but we have not discussed it. She is independent and her father says that she will marry when she wants.'

'What? But there must be someone?' Amma was aghast.

'Our holy book says a girl has a choice and forbids us to force her. She has graduated and her father wants her to

acquire a master's degree. So, she will study like boys do,' Shakoh's mother replied.

An air of deep desire filled Rafiq and his burdened house. He raised his head and saw Shakoh. As luminous as a full moon, she sat at the far end of their *takht*. He entered his room lit by the soft moonlight. Little did he know that his *dhanak* had followed him to his door. He looked at himself in the mirror and whispered, 'White clouds in my hair...'

'It's a starry sky to me. Who says that we can only fall in love with young beautiful faces and black hair? You should let a heart determined to love decide for itself.'

Rafiq Mian turned around in a daze. Shakoh, in bright green and black, was behind the curtain. She pushed the ashen drape between her cheek and hand, her feet visible under her sari, and said to Rafiq, 'Why are you so ashamed of a few white strands?'

His eyes did not waver from hers. She stepped out slowly as Rafiq watched her pink feet fade into the distance. His bedroom was redolent with the smell of her rose perfume and he thought of the many instances when Shakoh had conveyed her love for him. Shaukat's love had been evident in that lavish *dastarkhwan*. She also knew he liked firni and potato curry and that he would leave the table if the rice was thick.

The next day, Shakoh came out of the kitchen with bloodshot eyes. She called Hoori from the *aangan*, 'Hoori! Please see, is there something in my eyes?'

Rafiq came out of his room and saw Hoori scan Shakoh's eyes. Shaukat saw him and shrank back. 'Don't worry, I don't think we can find it.'

'Your eyes are large enough for a man to lose himself in,' Hoori quipped.

'What do you mean?'

'I mean Mamujaan fell into your eyes and got lost in them.'

'I hope I am never found,' said Rafiq softly. Shaukat lifted her lashes then shut her eyes to say she had captured him.

In the fragrant night, Rafiq lay awake in bed. His heart had regained its momentum. He thought about the days when his wedding had been a topic of conversation, now silenced by the silver streaks that cut through his dark hair – about telling Amma to ask for Shaukat's hand. She would leave in four days.

Amma came to his room during the day and said, 'Why don't you give these dirty clothes to the laundry?'

'I always forget, Amma.'

'It's covered in dust. Didn't you ask Baqar to clean? What must your clients think of you?'

'I have asked him but he is lazy.'

'Then get married!'

'Which girl will hold this old man's hand?'

Amma was furious. 'Old? Why don't you say you are about to die too?'

Rafiq laughed.

'A woman shows her love by caring for her man. Or else, a child would come into this world from a man's belly, not a womb.'

Rafiq sensed his cue and knew his rebirth was as clear as daylight. When he talked to Hoori, his eyes searched corridor to corridor for Shaukat, Shakoh's name often slipping from his lips.

'My name is Hoori. Your Shakoh is in the kitchen boiling potatoes,' his spirited niece retorted one time.

'Tell me if you agree, or they will leave. Shaukat insisted that they see your Apa during her vacations. Otherwise, we are no match for them,' said Amma.

'She came here for a few days. This cannot be the place for her marriage proposal. Why don't you write to her father after they leave?' Rafiq countered.

As those winter nights passed and the day of Shakoh and her mother's departure approached, the women made the most of their evenings together. The fireplace crackled with logs, cauldrons of tea simmered on stoves, *paans* and the hum of chatter went on into the night. One such night, Apa Bi stepped out to get some coal. Hit by the cold wind, she went back with a headache.

'What happened?' asked Amma.

'My head hurts. It's the breeze.'

In the morning, Apa ground the grains and cleaned the rice in the open. She washed utensils, then chopped the chillies. Slowly, her backache became severe and a day later she was stiff with torturous pain and high fever.

After the doctor left, Hoori sat beside her mother. 'Ammi, how do you feel now?'

Apa opened her eyes, smiled and comforted her daughter. 'I am well, but the headache is unbearable.'

'The house is so gloomy with you in bed,' Hoori moaned.

'Should I rub some balm on you, Ammi?'

'No, it ran out last night.'

'I will ask Zehra Mumani.'

Before Apa could stop her, she was in the *dalaan*, the foyer, and within a few moments, shrieks cut the air. Rafiq tried to listen. It was Zehra Dulhan.

'There is no pain. Shaukat Begum is leaving and Apa does not want to be in the kitchen.'

'She is in so much pain,' Hoori cried.

'Can pain be seen? Fever is another matter.'

'I asked for balm and you cursed me. It's a shame that you are a miser with Mamujaan's money. You don't have a penny of your own.'

The sound of hard slaps plunged into the darkness like daggers. 'Get out and don't set foot in this portion again,' thundered Annu.

Hoori ran to Rafiq. 'Mamujaan, I went to ask for balm and Mami insulted me. Chhote Mamu hit me six times.' She gripped him tightly, 'I am glad you aren't married or you would beat us too.'

'Don't cry, my Hoori… I am your loving mamu and I have never…' Rafiq could not complete his sentence. He just put a wrinkled hand on her head.

Rafiq Mian sank into despair. He felt like he was eighty; waxen face, hollow cheeks, his youthful abandon slayed. The truth that had chased him since his father's death had taken shape. As long as Hoori was in the house, the lamp of love he had come to live by would always be doused in his niece's tears. His defeated heart bled, a life of lost hope and loneliness was all he would have.

A cool breeze blew in from the veranda. Shaukat stared at Rafiq through a flimsy curtain. He put his hand on his chest, and in a low, trembling whisper, said, 'Amma, close this door.'

And with this, he knew he had shut the door on dreams of a life with Shaukat and every sensation of euphoria.

3

Nath ka Ghuroor

The Pride of a Nose ring

The elders cherished Shakoo and her genteel, orthodox family. A charming girl with illusions of romance, she never imagined that she could be seen as a saviour. But often a collage of dreams is the swansong of wonderment.

A famed matchmaker of Hyderabad, Jamila Bi, visited Maulvi Sahab's house. Shakoo's mother promptly told her daughter to go inside. Noble marriage brokers were astute readers of a family's essence and chose sincere families for Nawabs.

Jamila did not miss Shakoo's flight from the courtyard. She asked the mother about the age of her Bitiya Bi.

'Who, my Shakoo? She will be nineteen this year,' said the mother.

A worldly woman, she knew deceit well. She had seen mothers present women of twenty-five years as fifteen-year-olds. However, this was an honest home of a fair, comely, youthful college-going girl. Jamila Bi took out a paper from under her burqa, put on her glasses and read the virtues of a boy to the begum.

'He is dutiful, unpretentious and the heir to a royal clan. Nawabs have mistresses and decadent lifestyles. This boy is different, so I have been in search of a girl like your daughter. They will reward me well. Give your daughter's hand to this boy. He is a rare find. If you want, I can bring a picture,' she exclaimed.

Jamila Bi went to the Nawab's house and said the same about Shakoo. The two were soon engaged and then married.

Shakoo, the daughter of Maulvi Sahab, became the daughter-in-law of Lal Haveli. New brides were bestowed with titles, Afshan Dulhan, Khubsoorat Dulhan, Heera Dulhan, even Moti Dulhan. Begum Pasha, swayed by Jamila Bi's paeans, gave Shakoo the honour of Sharafat Dulhan.

With the honour came a heavy gold nose ring with five pearls and rubies. It hung from her delicate nostril and she was in pain.

'This is the beginning. What awaits you is tougher,' a lady lifted her veil and whispered mischievously.

She had heard about wild wedding nights from her friends. Some claimed that their grooms had wrenched their legs apart, others told sweeter tales of love.

It was three in the morning. She sat in her new bedroom, weighed down by anticipation, the jewels and her red regalia. Her back hurt and she felt her nose would weep with blood.

Then, she heard his footsteps; he was quiet as he hung up his large *sehra* and the turban, unbuttoned his sherwani and pushed his *saleem shahi* shoes aside. At the dawn of another life, she felt her heart leap and beat in her ears. He approached slowly and stood by the side of the bed. Shakoo froze.

He stammered. 'Sharafat Mahal, do you know what your nosepiece means? In our Lal Haveli, it makes you the keeper of this family's honour. This nose ring is the symbol of your respect for me.'

Shakoo's mind reeled from her mother's and her groom's words. Her nose ring felt heavier. It carried the dignity of two families.

'I know my sermon is far from pleasant but you are my wife and my honour. I don't deserve you. I cannot be with a woman. A long time ago, my life turned to rubble.' His voice was muffled, his eyes closed.

The walls tightened around her, so did each nerve in her body. She turned to look at herself in the mirror. Her finery jarred and she sniffled. Shakoo scoured through her life in

the desperate search for a sin that made her unworthy of a spirited future.

'Now you are mine so I can tell you my darkest secret.' He opened his eyes and turned her face towards his. She was an image of gloom. Her face as red as the arc of fire around a setting sun, kohl-lined eyes filled with unspoken words, and parched lips.

'Please don't look at me like this,' he begged.

Shakoo saw a man with a loutish air, as unappealing to look at as a rotting corpse. She recalled the time when Jamila Bi brought his photograph. Her friends had scoffed at his moustache and her first thought was that he was an ailing man with black rings around his eyes.

'My name is Nawab Wajahat. It means a handsome man. Many women came to my bedroom, but a bitch in this haveli made me lifeless,' he said, his face as red as hers. She listened in silence.

'You come from a simple family, unaware of the truths buried in a haveli. If a maid is favoured by the father, his sons can enjoy her. It is not a secret. Everyone can drink from the same tap.' The new bride broke into a sweat, but he continued.

'This bitch with a full bosom was an outrageous flirt. When the men teased her and said, "What is under your shirt?" she replied, "Do you want me to lift it for you?" Sometimes she would say, "It is the milk of the child I will

bear you."' As Wajahat Nawab spoke of his scandal in a monotone, Shakoo turned a pasty white.

'One day, I asked her if she really wanted to feed a child. She pulled me to her bed and laid me down. Then, she tempted me. 'Why just the child? Why not the father?' She drew her shirt up and shoved her nipple into my mouth. After that, I went limp. When I try to arouse myself, I fail.'

Naked grief ran through Shakoo's every vein, making her disconsolate.

'Cry as much as you want. You cannot share this with anyone.' He picked up a cluster of keys from the table and placed them in her lap. 'These are the keys to my locker. You can have whatever you want. Anyone else in my place would tell you about his impotence in the same way,' he said.

Her state made him repentant. Wajahat explained that he was overwhelmed by his parents, who wanted an heir for the estate from him. He had tried to seize every chance to speak to them, but the shame crippled him.

'So I thought if I don't have children, they will presume my wife is infertile.'

'Don't say that,' cried Shakoo. She wept, crashing her head against the headboard. It did not stop him.

'I told the matchmaker to find a pious bride for me. When she told us about you and your mother, I knew my sad truth would be safe with an innocent girl. My mother had to obey. People listen to me and fear me.'

She looked at him intently and then remembered an old Deccan saying, 'Whether a wife is faithful or not, for the world she will always be as loyal as a dog and that too without any doubt.'

Nawab put his turban at her feet. 'I beg you, don't force me to make love to you because I can't do it.'

She recoiled. At once disgusted and full of pity at the surrender of a powerful man. The desire of a fervent bride, her body wet with a new smell, was stifled by the certainty of celibacy for life.

Many suns rose on the horizon, with Lal Haveli's women chatting about motherhood and doting on their babies. Each day faded in the blaze of ceremonies – from *bismillah*, birthdays to circumcisions. Sharafat Dulhan became as uneasy as her husband was on their wedding night.

In keeping with the palace tradition, bejewelled daughters-in-law came to Begum's door to greet her, and she said a prayer for their husbands.

'May your husband live long and have many children.' Sharafat Dulhan would shudder at every word.

When the family gathered around a meal, sweet-and-sour pickles were laid out for new brides. 'Serve the pickle to them. They will be too shy to ask in front of everyone!' Begum ordered. Gradually, Sharafat disappeared from the dining table.

Nawab Sakhawat Yar Jung, Wajahat's father, had built

a mosque in the vast grounds of the haveli. The clan came together for prayers and the women lined up in the last row. Whenever Shakoo spent a week away from the mosque, Ammi Huzoor grieved.

'So, this month too Dulhan missed her prayers!' she would say to the ladies of her manor.

The lands of Sakhawat Jung were in Shadnagar, where Nawab Wajahat lived for most months of the year. His absence made his mother seethe.

'You must have a baby with Dulhan! Why are you leaving again?' she would fume at him.

Nawab Wajahat returned to Lal Haveli after several months. Terrified of his temper and unforgiving attitude towards the staff and his younger siblings, most scurried into corners. His brothers and their wives crept to their rooms.

When he found cobwebs in various nooks, he thundered, 'When will you clean the haveli?' He berated gardeners for the lack of seasonal blooms and warned the epicene staff about the dust on chandeliers and carpets. Then, the frail state of the horses brought his wrath on the horsemen.

As washed up as he was, Sharafat Dulhan had begun to understand and even share his discomfort. However, she was loved in Lal Haveli.

This time, when Nawab Wajahat left for Shadnagar, Dulhan was weak with a headache. One of the hijras entered her room to light the chandelier.

'May I help you, Dulhan Pasha?' asked the tall, well-built Mehmood Bi.

'Shabratan, Chameli, Sanober, Gulshan, there are many to help me. You go and light the lamps,' Shakoo smiled.

'I know they help you, but you seem unwell.'

Mehmood Bi untied Dulhan's hair and a black cascade fell to the floor. 'You tied up your wet hair, so now you have a headache. Let me steam it with *oudh*, you will feel better.'

'Let me be, Mehmood Bi. The smoke from my charred heart will dry it,' sighed Dulhan.

When Mehmood Bi put her hand on Sharafat's forehead, for a second she felt the touch of a man.

'Are you a hijra?' she asked.

Mehmood Bi flinched. 'No. You are educated so I will not lie, but no one knows. I am poor and had no choice. The haveli pays well. We are given gifts and ample food.'

'You are not ashamed to dress and behave this way?' asked Dulhan.

He lowered his head silently.

'Are you married?'

'No, I have two young sisters. They must get married before I think about myself. My mother does not know about my job. I go home in a churidar pyjama, kurta and *saleem shahi* shoes.'

Surprised by his candour and at having a man in her chambers, Sharafat Dulhan raised her head and gave him a

once-over. A wild thought crossed her mind. Mehmood was handsome and would probably appear masculine if he were to undress.

'You can go now. I am sleepy,' she said, turning to the side.

By the time their second wedding anniversary came, younger couples were with their infants and Begum Pasha was heartbroken for her eldest son. Shakoo overheard her sharing her grief with the family. 'Shaukat Pasha and Raza Pasha got married after Wajahat Pasha. They are fathers but not Wajahat.'

A few days later, Begum revealed her new plan. 'I am thinking about Wajahat's second marriage. After all, people marry many times to have children. Our son can afford to marry fifty times.'

'Then who has stopped you?' asked her sister. 'Wait for this month to end. I have Asmat Yar Jung's granddaughter in mind for him.'

'But will they give their granddaughter as a second wife?'

'I will tell them that their granddaughter will be our Bahu Huzoor and Sharafat Begum the caretaker of the child.'

Their plan made Sharafat Mahal spiteful. After the night's prayer, she sent for Mehmood Bi.

'Mehmood Bi, did you light the lamps tonight?' she asked, stretched out on the bed.

The lamps were aglow. Mehmood Bi was surprised by her query. He looked at Dulhan Pasha and turned to lock

the door. When she moaned, he strode towards her like a lightning bolt.

In the morning, Dulhan, dewy and languid, stayed in bed. Her blankets, pillows and bed sheet were tangled and soaked in the scent of their night together. A while later, she got up and washed the sheets herself.

This time, Nawab Wajahat returned after ten months, during which there had been no news from him. Although he did not send letters, tidings from the family reached him through his servants. His personal valet told Nawab, 'I will take a gold chain from you worth a hundred and one rupees.'

'Why?' asked Wajahat Yar Jung.

'You have become a father,' he replied.

Scalded by the revelation, he raced to Lal Haveli on horseback. A lavish celebration was held with a feast, music and plaudits from the guests. Wajahat met his ecstatic Ammi Huzoor, received blessings from his relatives and bounded up to his room, where Sharafat Dulhan cradled her baby.

'Close the door,' she said. 'I am feeding the baby.'

'What is all this?' He bristled.

'This is your infant,' she replied, pointing to the baby. He stomped towards it with clenched fists, but she halted him with a gesture.

'Let me explain. I am Shakira, the woman who wore this nose ring. Your mother thought of a second wife for you. Tell me, how will you be with another woman? Will she keep

your secret and respect you? You know all your property will go to your family. Listen, you played the field and were with many women. But who will think of me? Why should I be sentenced to death for your inability to be a man to his woman? Like Eve, I have tasted the forbidden fruit. You can turn me out if you want. If you do, your mother will bring another bride,' she said with unvarnished, cold bluntness.

The nose ring sparkled as Nawab Wajahat stood motionless, wedged between betrayal and brilliance.

4

Naulakha Haar

The Necklace

It was only one night for Dulhan Pasha. She lived with it and longed to sway with rapture. Her daughter, Tara, tame like the first dapples of spring sun, was a whit more sensitive than dead wood.

Last night was *ratjaga*, celebrations that continued nightlong. The mansion was heavy-eyed in the morning; its quiet cut into with sounds of a lady cracking betel nuts in the ornate foyer. She yelled at the listless maids, 'Lazy whores, when will you wake up? It's the mehndi tonight!' and turned back to her nutcracker. Meanwhile, Dulhan was sleepless.

'Mughlani Amma, is Bibi Tara's dupatta trimmed with lace?' she asked softly.

'Yes, but there is so much left for these indolent women. Pasha, you haven't slept a wink. Go and rest or you will ruin your health.'

Dulhan Pasha was quiet.

'I know the marriage of a daughter is far from easy till the nikah,' Mughlani Amma sighed.

Dulhan cut her short. 'No, Mughlani Amma, my health is fine. I took a long nap.'

'Good nap?' The old lady guffawed knowingly.

Ever since her second day in the grandiose palace, a structure that dominated the skyline of Hyderabad Deccan, restful sleep had been an elusive dream for Dulhan.

Although there were many impressive weddings, her father made hers a dazzling festival of splendour that lasted for weeks. After all, she was the only sister of her three brothers. It was a ceremony imprinted on the city's landscape, a wedding worth a thousand weddings.

Nawab Sahab chose the most striking suitor in Nawab Daulat Yar Jung, who came in princely wonder – jewelled turban, star-strewn sherwani, brocade churidar pyjama and a *sehra* down to his feet. Ashrafi was brought amid eddies of light. He swept her up like she was a petal, the only time Dulha Mian held his wife.

Dulhan Pasha's family named their daughter Ashrafi Bano because she was as radiant as gold. Ladies of the haveli were forbidden to make eye contact and Ashrafi's almond eyes were always downcast. It was also home to another strange custom, whereby girls remained bare under their kurtas.

Soon after the first dawn of Dulhan's marriage broke, she, hot as flames of sulphur, began to fall into slow decay. Dulha Pasha had stepped out and strolled into the garden, where a tumultuous scene played out. A girl was berating a frightened gardener.

'Girl, why are you making so much noise?' asked the Nawab, appalled.

She turned to him and bowed her head. He was overwhelmed by the spark in her eyes, her mouth spewed nectar and she had a body as plump as a Roman sculpture.

'Do I look like a girl to you?' she shot back.

'Yes. Men don't have peaks like yours.'

'Call me by my name, Sarkar.'

'What is your name?' he asked, swallowing a laugh.

'Bagia.'

'Bagia, a garden? I can see your flowers,' he said flirtatiously.

Hearing him allude to flowers, the unnerved gardener intervened. 'Sarkar, I told her that no one is allowed to pluck flowers. She insisted on a bouquet for Bibi Sahab.'

She dismissed him. 'I have seen many guardians of flowers like you. Go to your own Bibi's lehenga.'

Bagia was one of many maids who had accompanied Dulhan. An outspoken, tall nomad from the south, she was the personal *baandhi*, the maid who regaled Ashrafi with her wit and effervescence.

Dulha Pasha's loins had never known such heat. Bagia's raw, fleshy appeal stirred his violent hunger for her. She arched, churned and pulled with electric vigour till a sudden dullness came over him, as if he had been poisoned. He eventually became as flaccid as a wilted flower. The man who lifted the bride like a feather was now trembling with a glass of water in his hand.

Dulhan Pasha's adolescence became riddled with despair. Gripping the memory of their only night together, she became a mother at fifteen. Little Bibi Tara was the centrepiece of her life. Dulhan Begum turned her back on the legion of staff and lived as her baby's playmate and nanny.

Bibi Tara grew up to be beautiful. At eleven, she dressed in her mother's dowry clothes and called Dulhan Apa. When the swings came out in monsoons, the two rocked in the courtyard, played hide-and-seek and *aankh micholi*, the classic Indian blindfold game.

When Tara was not at school, she was being groomed to preside over a house. Friends with the maids, she was as quick as a wink at grasping the etiquettes of hosting and ceremonies.

Nawab Daulat Yar Jung wanted to bequeath his fortune to his only child. A tidal wave of marriage proposals flowed in as soon as she turned sixteen. The idea of parting with her gnawed at her mother's soul. Tara was Dulhan Pasha's sole possession.

Although their marriage was a mantle of death splattered with rare words from Nawab Daulat, she approached her husband to discuss Tara.

'You are the father and whatever you decide will be accepted. But please look for a son-in-law who will live with us.'

'How will we get such a son-in-law?' he asked.

'Anyone who receives so much from you will be happy to stay here. I cannot live without my daughter.' Dulhan dissolved into tears.

'God willing, it will be according to your wishes,' replied Nawab. He found a touch of atonement in his compliance.

A few months later, Bibi Tara sat for the rites of her wedding, which began with a *mayyun*, the haldi ceremony. But the *ratjaga* wafted Dulhan away like a tornado. Every wound opened and bled inside her.

Heaters and stoves on Shahabadi stones simmered with gulgule, chongay, meway ki poorian, malida for guests, and

wedding singers broke into ballads laced with risqué lyrics. Away from the riotous cheer in the palace, Dulhan spent the night in her room.

'My throat is dry. I need some rest. Someone else should take over,' complained a singer.

'Let's play a game of riddles,' a maid quipped.

'The one who loses will be my slave,' said a cousin with a laugh.

'Here we go. I have many riddles. *Ek thaal motiyon bhara, sab ke sar par ondha padachaaron orr woh thaal phiray, moti uss se ek na giray.* (A plate full of pearls, flipped over the heads of all, when spun around in circles, not one pearl fell from it).'

'It's so easy! The sky and the stars,' screamed the jubilant women.

'Yes! Now one more,' said another maid.

'*Chataakh pataakh kab se? Haath pakda jab se. Aah ooyi kab se? Aadha gaya jab se. Chup chaap kab se? Saara gaya jab se.* When did the twisting and crashing start? Since the hand was first held. What about the ahhing and oohing? When it was half in. And since when was there silence? Since it was all in!'

The women teased the maid in the boisterous courtyard.

'What can I say! You have filthy minds. It's Amir Khusro's famous riddle. The answer is a bracelet,' she said sharply.

'So, another. *Baat ki baat tutoli ki tutoli, mard ki gaanth aurat ne kholi.* Word for word, search and search, a woman undoes a man's knot.

'A padlock,' came Bibi Tara's perfect reply.

'I have one and whoever cannot solve it will be my servant,' said Tara's friend.

'Go ahead.'

'*Sote sote, haath mein le kar soye.* It's held in the hand while sleeping.'

'You slut, you have a dirty mind.'

'I'll ask another, but both riddles have the same answer. Listen carefully.'

'*Asalta masalta, hath main lo toh phisalta.* It twists and turns, but will slip if you take it in your hand.'

And pat came Tara's response, 'A hand fan for both riddles.'

'If any of you can't guess mine then a hundred sit-ups for you,' joked Mughlani Amma's married daughter.

'*Arodo marodo, thook laga kar andar ghusado.* Turn it, twist it, and to slip it in moisten with spit.'

There were whispers among the women, then a girl ran out and returned with something in her hand.

'A thread and a needle,' she shouted.

The ladies lay into her for being a cheat. She closed the book of riddles that she'd snuck in earlier and said, 'I promise, I will not cheat. But everyone should play fair.'

'Bibi Tara, ask something!' her friends urged, giggling, tickling her.

'I will say one riddle and none after that.'

She looked at her hand, smiled. '*Tu jaata tha, main pukarti thi, tu daalta tha main roti thi.* I cried out when you departed and I cried when you put it in.'

At that moment, Dulhan Pasha burst out of her room, which opened into the courtyard.

'What is this rubbish! There are unmarried girls here.'

Bibi was stunned at her mother's rage. 'Apa, it's the bangle seller, the *chudiwala*.'

The frightened young girl gave her book to Dulhan Pasha. 'You can see, Pasha, we have learnt these from this book.'

Dulhan paused, snatched the book and returned to her room. It said, 'Some Deccani Riddles by Muhammad Naeem-ur-Rehman, M.A. from Allahabad'. She went through it. Every evocative word brought back memories of loneliness. The torrent of a parched past, days and nights, as if tied to her by an umbilical cord, collapsed on her. She tore it up page by page. Dulhan thought of the time when she had walked out to the garden on a night of lightning and lashing rain. Soaked and cold, she had returned to an empty room and a quilt to keep her warm. Then there was the instance when her brother-in-law, Shaukat Nawab, had pulled her dupatta from her chest and she'd slapped him in the face.

For all these years, only slabs of ice in her bath water

had cooled her youthful, sensuous body. Her mind became a womb of moments, which spoke to her of Nawab Daulat Yar Jang's desertion and mocked her unassuming, artless demeanour when men in the mansion eyed her.

Deafened by the cruelty of her memories, she covered her ears. 'It's my child's marriage. And even though I am a thirty-two-year-old with desires, I will be a mother-in-law. My time is behind me.' She moaned, sat up and clasped her chest.

The *ratjaga* and mehndi were done, and it was Tara's wedding day. The groom was to live with them; a fine choice, but thirty-four years of age.

'Apa, we had to compromise. He is perfect in every other way,' consoled her friends.

'When she is a mother, Tara will look older. The age difference will not matter,' said others, comforting her. However, the sceptics outnumbered the sympathizers.

Nawab Rafat crossed the threshold. A lean, flamboyant young man with bright eyes, he did not look a day past twenty-five. His regal baraat brought a *naulakha haar,* an heirloom necklace worth nine hundred thousand rupees, for the bride.

While their nikah was sanctified, the band rolled with the beats of the dholak to announce the marriage. It was time for the first glance, the *arsee musaf*, after which the groom

would carry the bride into the room. Bibi Tara, in luxuriant Hyderabadi wraps, *teeka, jhoomar, karanphool* and *hathphool*, shone like a gilded crimson gemstone.

Dulhan Pasha chose a bridal chamber next to hers. The bride was led to their wide, canopied bed of silver. She sat in the middle, with her mother beside her. Rafat entered his new bedroom and took a seat near Tara. He heard a *meerasan*, one of the wedding singers, say, 'Dulhan Pasha also looks like a bride.'

He stared, rapt in his mother-in-law's allure. An appealing woman, majestic in demeanour, sublime in beauty. Traditionally, mothers-in-law covered their faces in front of their sons-in-law. A gold-rimmed mirror arrived; the groom turned his gaze towards it, saw his luminous bride and raised the *naulakha haar* to her neck.

A woman remarked, 'She is laden with jewellery. It's such a heavy piece! You can put it on her later.'

'What should I do with it?' he asked impishly.

'Give it to Dulhan Begum. Take it when you want. Put it around her neck for now,' she replied.

When Rafat Mian leaned forward to put the necklace on the anxious Dulhan, he saw her cleavage and grinned.

After the groom's ceremonies ended, it was the turn of Nawab Daulat Yar Jung's family turn to present *salaami* and *muh dikhai*. The women in the room watched over every

step with instructions and commentary. 'Give gold bangles to Tara and five gold coins to Dulha Mian. He gave Tara a necklace and she gave him a watch.'

Dulhan Pasha's burnished dupatta overwhelmed him with its vibrance and delicate golden web. The customs began to tire him. Rafat's head spun in a vortex of hues, lustre, beauty and imagery. He had to chase his thoughts away; her garb merely veiled his truth.

Dulhan Begum stood up. 'I'm going to my room.' She left, but stayed in his mind.

After a memorable meal, a slow silence fell over the haveli. Guests, *baraatis* and servants, all called it a night.

For years, Dulhan Pasha had watched dark nights die at daybreak, and that night she went to her bed on an empty stomach. The burden of thirty-two years was heavier; she unfurled her hair, as black as her fate. Sanober had steamed it with fragrance that morning. She placed her dupatta near the pillow and closed the patio door. The door from her room to Bibi Tara's was shut but unbolted.

Dulhan's only night with her husband had been their wedding night. Their first moments together drifted to her mind. Nawab Sahab had asked her for a *paan*, and she had fed it to him with her henna-filigreed hands. He had sucked it into his mouth and then engulfed her body with his.

Tied to her fears and a fairytale wish for Tara, she went to their room to see if the silver *paandaan* was in place.

Begum entered and tripped over a cushion. Rafat was taking his socks off on the side. Dulhan Pasha had left her dupatta on the bedside, and her taut frame turned the groom into a famished beast.

Then, in a deep voice dipped in hot honey, he said, 'The necklace looks beautiful on you' – and she was on the velvet bedspread, her body fresh with rapture.

Dulhan's memory of that night was faint. Its traces in her mind as shadowy as a water-colour painting in the rain. It was four in the morning, and she lay naked. She sprang up, lunged at Rafat, pounded him with her fists and then tried to strangle him. In her ferocity, Rafat saw a wildly alluring woman. She made him quake with violent convulsions.

'You animal! You bloody monster! You have destroyed my daughter. May God never give you happiness.'

The next day, Dulhan remained in her room. Bibi Tara's friends and cousins flocked to the bridal room, seeking every snippet of her passionate time. The bride, as pure as a young leaf, and unacquainted with the intimacies of a wedding night, giggled.

Dulhan Pasha woke up in the late afternoon. She was nailed to her bed by her sin. A few hours later, she trudged to the bathroom with a torn heart. She wore a yellow kurta and pyjama, wrapped a dupatta around her head, and stood on the prayer rug for the Asr prayer. Then she slammed her head on the ground with a desperate appeal. 'God, please

forgive me! I am stained with an inconceivable sin. Give me death!'

At night, Dulhan Pasha came to the dinner table where a stunned household glared at her new radiance. The groom's greeting was tinged with remorse.

'He is only two years older than you,' a lady rasped in her ear.

'No, he is my son-in-law,' she snapped.

Dadi Huzoor feared that Dulha Mian may have been too wilful with Tara. She asked the maids to take the bride to rest and told Rafat to spend the night alone.

Midnight melted into one, and then two, in the morning. A dim shaft of blue light flickered from under the door. Every moment stung Dulhan as Bibi Tara slept in her grandmother's arms.

Gusts of wind carried the scent of jasmine as she let her hair down. Then, like a sleepwalker, she stealthily went to Rafat's room and pushed his door open.

'You?' he gushed, his eyes lit with longing.

'I am wearing the *naulakha haar* again.'

Acknowledgements

This journey began with the kind Mohammad Zahid in Urdu Bazar, Lahore. His knowledge, time and determination to find Wajida Tabassum's stories for me will remain an invaluable treasure.

Gazi Khan, Wajida Tabassum's son in Mumbai, India, who was located after two long months of chasing clues and making calls to bewildered people in various parts of the globe. A reporter finds it difficult to let a story go and I finally reached him at 3 a.m. on email via a contact in the Middle East. His prompt, unconditional permission to me to translate his mother's works was the best outcome ever.

Kanishka Gupta, my dear friend, literary agent and founder of Writer's Side, for not tearing his hair out at the many onslaughts of my nervous energy, queries and panic.

Suhayb Alvi, senior culture columnist and media professional, who was integral to this compilation as a medium to decipher the original Deccani Urdu text.

The small treasure of friends who never left my side.

Imran Aslam, my uncle and president of Geo Television and Jang Group, for his most poetic mind and support.

Poulomi Chatterjee, for being the beautiful person she is and her immeasurable generosity. Swarnima Narayan, a real pleasure of an editor, for her sparkling ideas, perception, cooperation and encouragement. The intense, immaculate cover for this book comes from Pia Alize Hazarika, and captures the mood, ambience, themes of the stories with uncanny precision and beauty. Working with Hachette India has been an experience to cherish. This book is theirs first.